She took another glance at the puppy thief holding her Yorkie mix and melted a little bit. The two of them looked like they belonged on that Instagram account her dancer friends were always going on about—Hot Men and Mutts.

She swallowed. "Look, is there any way we could work this out ourselves before the shelter manager gets involved? The puppy is a gift. Couldn't you just pick out another one? I love that dog. What can I do to change your mind? Anything?"

Surely there was something he wanted, although Chloe couldn't imagine what it might be.

She lifted her chin and looked him directly in his eyes, so he'd know she meant business. No reindeer games.

Then she tilted her head, prompting him to say something. Anything.

Make me an offer.

His gaze narrowed and sharpened. For a second or two, he focused on her with such intensity that she forgot how to breathe.

So there is *something he wants, after all.*

When at last he gave her the answer she'd been waiting for, he didn't crack a smile.

"Marry me."

* * *

WILDE HEARTS:
Letting their hearts loose, one Wilde at a time!

Dear Reader,

Happy holidays!

Christmas is my favorite time of year and there's no place quite like New York during the holidays, so I'm happy to bring you a sweet story set in the Big Apple.

The opening of this book takes place at an animal shelter and is filled with Christmas cheer, including our heroine, Chloe Wilde, dressed in a bedazzled reindeer costume. It's a whimsical romance, but it's also about a man dealing with grief and learning how to be a father to his five-year-old niece after her world has been turned upside down. Plagued by guilt and desperate to secure custody of Lolly, Anders Kent is in need of a Christmas miracle. He never suspects his guardian angel might just come dressed as Rudolph.

A Daddy by Christmas is the fourth and final book in my Wilde Hearts series. I've loved writing about this family, their charming brownstone, the Bennington Hotel and the Wilde family dance school in the West Village. I hope you've enjoyed cheering for each of the Wildes as they've found love and happiness in the city that never sleeps.

If this is your first Wilde Hearts read, don't worry! Each book can be read as a stand-alone. But I hope you'll check out the other books in the series—*The Ballerina's Secret*, *How to Romance a Runaway Bride* and *The Bachelor's Baby Surprise*.

Wishing you happy reading and a very merry Christmas,

Teri Wilson

A Daddy by Christmas

Teri Wilson

HARLEQUIN® SPECIAL EDITION

ISBN-13: 978-1-335-46618-1

A Daddy by Christmas

This edition published by arrangement with Harlequin Books S.A.

For questions and comments about the quality of this book, please contact us at CustomerService@Harlequin.com.

Printed in U.S.A.

Teri Wilson is a novelist for Harlequin. She is the author of *Unleashing Mr. Darcy*, now a Hallmark Channel Original Movie. Teri is also a contributing writer at hellogiggles.com, a lifestyle and entertainment website founded by Zooey Deschanel that is now part of the *People* magazine, *Time* magazine and *Entertainment Weekly* family. Teri loves books, travel, animals and dancing every day. Visit Teri at teriwilson.net or on Twitter, @teriwilsonauthr.

Books by Teri Wilson

Harlequin Special Edition

Wilde Hearts

The Ballerina's Secret
How to Romance a Runaway Bride
The Bachelor's Baby Surprise

Drake Diamonds

His Ballerina Bride
The Princess Problem
It Started with a Diamond

HQN Books

Unmasking Juliet
Unleashing Mr. Darcy

Visit the Author Profile page
at Harlequin.com for more titles.

In loving memory of my dad, Bob Wilson.

Chapter One

The puppy was the last straw.

Chloe Wilde's bad luck streak kicked off a little over a week ago while performing with the Rockettes during the annual Thanksgiving Day parade. She'd taken a tumble and accidentally ruined the dance troupe's legendary toy soldier routine on live television. Things had progressed from bad to worse ever since, and now, just twenty-four days before Christmas, she'd reached rock bottom.

"I don't understand." One of the sequined antlers on Chloe's glittering derby hat drooped into her line of vision and she pushed it away, aiming her fiercest glower at the woman who'd just given her the bad news. Not that glowering while dressed as a high-kicking reindeer was an easy task. It wasn't, but after everything Chloe had been through lately, she excelled at it. “I’ve been visiting this puppy every day for twelve days. I filled out an adoption application a week ago, and you yourself called me last night and told me I’d been approved.”

That phone call had been the first good thing that had happened to her in *days*. Weeks, if she was really being honest with herself. But that was okay, because starting today, she wouldn’t have to face the worst Christmas of her adult life by herself. She’d have a snuggly, adorable puppy by her side.

Or so she thought.

The man standing beside Chloe cleared his throat. “She called me yesterday afternoon and told me the same thing.”

“Just because she called you first doesn’t mean the puppy is yours.” Chloe took a time-out from her refusal to acknowledge the man’s presence to glare at him.

She wished he weren’t so handsome. Those piercing blue eyes were a little difficult to ignore, as was his perfect square jaw. His clothes were impeccable—very tailored, very Wall Street. And the dusting of snow on the shoulders of his dark wool coat made him seem ultramanly for some reason. Under normal circumstances, she’d have thought he looked like the kind of man who would turn up wielding a little blue box in a Tiffany’s Christmas advertisement.

But these weren’t normal circumstances, and he wasn’t holding a little blue box. He was holding a puppy. *Her* puppy.

"Actually, that's exactly what it means. She called me first, and a verbal agreement was made wherein I would take possession of the puppy." He arched a brow. "Therefore the puppy is mine."

Who talked like that?

Chloe turned her back to him and refocused her attention on the animal shelter's adoption counselor, who thus far hadn't been much help. But Chloe wasn't going down without a fight.

"Are you really going to let him take my puppy? Listen to him. He says he wants to adopt a pet, but he sounds like he's talking about a business merger."

The adoption counselor's gaze swiveled back and forth between the two of them as if she were watching a snowball fight.

"She's not your dog. I'm adopting her. I've got the papers right here." Using his free hand, the man pulled an envelope from the inside pocket of his suit jacket and placed it on the counter.

Chloe didn't bother opening it. Instead, she pulled an identical packet of papers from her dance bag and slammed it on the counter next to his envelope.

"I've got papers, too." She crossed her arms, causing the jingle bell cuffs on the long brown velvet sleeves of her costume to clang, echoing loudly in the tiled shelter lobby.

The man's mouth twitched into a half grin, which, to Chloe's dismay, made him even more attractive. "Nice outfit, by the way."

She jammed her hands on her velvet-clad hips, ignoring the jingly commotion she made every time she moved. "I'll have you know that this is an official Rockettes reindeer costume, steeped in Christmas tradition dating back to the 1930s. I'm basically a New York treasure. So laugh it up, puppy thief."

He cut his gaze toward her, and his smile faded. "Once again, I'm not a puppy thief."

"Says the man who refuses to let go of my puppy." Chloe cast a longing glance at the tiny Yorkie mix. "You know who you are? You're Cruella De Vil in pinstripes."

"Pinstripes haven't been in style in years," he muttered.

"Note taken, Cruella."

"You know what?" The adoption counselor finally chimed in. "I think I should probably go get the manager so she can help us figure out how to proceed."

"Excellent. Thank you so much." Chloe nodded. Out of the corner of her eye, she could see the twinkle lights on her antlers blinking.

Oops. She could have sworn she'd switched those off.

Her nemesis turned toward her. Chloe still didn't quite trust herself to look at him without swooning, but she couldn't keep pretending he was invisible when they were the only two people in the room.

His gaze flitted to her antlers. "Are you really a Rockette?"

"Yes." She nodded. *Jingle, jingle, jingle.*

"That's quite impressive."

"Thank you." She cleared her throat.

It wasn't a lie. Not technically.

On paper, she was still a Rockette. She just wasn't allowed to perform anymore. Much to her humiliation, she now had the lovely task of standing in Times Square in her reindeer costume two hours a day to hand out flyers to tourists to encourage them to go to the annual Rockettes Christmas show at Radio City Music Hall.

Oh, how the mighty had fallen.

For the past four years, she'd been living her dream. She'd high-kicked her way through the last four Christmases—three shows a day for five weeks straight. Twice, she'd even traveled overseas with the Rockettes to perform in their USO tour. And now she'd been relegated to Times Square. She might as well put on an Elmo costume and a Santa hat and call it a day.

The worst part about being demoted wasn't the humiliation, nor was it the drastically reduced paycheck. Although she was going to have to do something about the latter really soon.

More troubling than either her dwindling bank account or her shame at the 50,000-plus YouTube views of her Thanksgiving Day toy soldier mishap was the prospect of telling her family she was no longer dancing. The Wildes weren't a scary bunch. Quite the opposite, actually. They were loving and supportive, especially Chloe's mother, Emily, who'd started the Wilde School of Dance over forty years ago and still taught nearly every day.

As much as Chloe hated to admit it, she'd taken advantage of all that family devotion. She'd used her busy rehearsal schedule as an excuse to miss nearly all the weekly dinners at the Wilde brownstone for the past few years. Every Thanksgiving and every Christmas, she'd been too busy performing at the parade or at Radio City to be a part of the family holiday celebrations. She couldn't even remember the last time she'd set foot in the dance school.

Her brother and sister liked to joke about it, calling her the ghost of Christmas past, but her mom never complained. No one had, even though Chloe knew she could have made more of an effort. What had she been thinking? Hadn't her dad's sudden death from a heart attack taught her not to take family for granted?

She was a horrible person. She couldn't even bring herself to tell the Wildes the truth. No wonder fate had thrown a puppy thief into her path. She deserved this, didn't she?

Her gaze slid toward the dog's scruffy little face and her tiny button nose. So adorable. Somehow her cuteness seemed magnified in the arms of Chloe's strapping rival.

She felt her chin start to wobble.

Stay strong.

The only thing that would make this episode more upsetting would be if she broke down and cried.

"Were you telling the truth just now? Have you actually visited this dog every day for the past twelve days?"

She peered up at the man and squared her shoulders. "Yes. Did you think I was lying?"

Chloe would never lie to the adoption counselor's

face like that. Lies of omission were apparently her thing, specifically lying by omission to her own flesh and blood.

He sighed and said nothing in response.

Chloe's heart gave a little zing. Was he beginning to crack?

"I already bought her a dog bed," Chloe said. "It's red-and-white-striped, like a candy cane."

"I wouldn't expect anything else from a woman dressed as Rudolph." His frown stayed firmly in place, but Chloe thought she spotted a twinkle in his eyes that hadn't been there before.

He was either about to give in and let her have the puppy, or he was flirting with her in order to get her to throw in the towel. For a second, Chloe wasn't sure which scenario she preferred.

She blinked.

Had she lost her mind? She wasn't going to let a few kind words and an eye twinkle crack her composure. Even if the eye twinkle was just shy of a full-on smolder.

That puppy was hers.

"Nice try," she said tartly. "But I'm not here to play games."

"No reindeer games." He gave her a solemn nod. "Got it."

The man was hardly playing fair, damn him.

"Good," she said.

Then she looked away, lest he see the smile on her face.

An awkward silence fell between them, punctuated every so often by the bells on Chloe's costume. She tried her best to keep her gaze focused on the countertop and the adoption papers she'd filled out in careful handwriting the night before. But the puppy started making cute little whimpering noises, and she couldn't help it. She had to look.

The tiny dog was gnawing on the handsome man's thumb, which would have been completely adorable if he'd been paying any attention whatsoever to the animal. He wasn't, though. His brow was furrowed, and he was staring into space, distracted.

Chloe rolled her eyes. He was probably thinking about the stock market or suing someone or the recent demise of pinstripes. "Why do you want this dog, anyway? You don't really seem like the Yorkie type."

He glanced at the dog and then at her. "What type do I seem like?"

A golden retriever, maybe. Or an Irish setter. A classic sort of dog that would look good curled in front of a fireplace or with its head sticking out of a town car.

"I haven't given it any thought," she lied.

He peered at her for a long, loaded moment, as if he could see inside her head. Finally, he said, "The puppy is an early Christmas gift."

"A *Christmas gift*?" Chloe blinked in indignation. "Do the people here at the shelter know that? Pets are living creatures. You can't just give them away as presents. That's the height of irresponsibility."

He shifted the puppy to his other arm, farther away

from her. “Rest assured, the shelter staff knows. I’m taking full responsibility for the dog.”

“So…what, then? She’s a gift for your wife?” Chloe’s gaze flitted to his left hand.

No ring.

“No wife,” he said. Then he frowned, as if his bachelorhood was a surprise. Or a problem that needed to be fixed.

Chloe’s face went hot for reasons she didn’t care to contemplate.

She took a deep breath. Action was required. If she didn’t stop thinking about this mysterious man’s relationship status and *do* something, she’d be going home to an empty apartment, complete with an empty candy cane–striped dog bed.

Her own bed would be empty, too, but that was fine. Preferable, actually. Although why she was suddenly thinking about the unoccupied half of her antique sleigh bed was a mystery.

Sure it is.

She took another glance at the puppy thief holding her Yorkie mix and melted a little bit. The two of them looked like they belonged on that Instagram account her dancer friends were always going on about—Hot Men and Mutts.

She swallowed. “Look, is there any way we could work this out ourselves before the shelter manager gets involved? The puppy is a gift. Couldn’t you just pick out another one? I love that dog. What can I do to change your mind? Anything?”

Surely there was something he wanted, although Chloe couldn't imagine what it might be.

She lifted her chin and looked him directly in his eyes, so he'd know she meant business. No reindeer games.

Then she tilted her head, prompting him to say something. Anything.

Make me an offer.

His gaze narrowed and sharpened. For a second or two, he focused on her with such intensity that she forgot how to breathe.

So there is *something he wants, after all.*

When at last he gave her the answer she'd been waiting for, he didn't crack a smile.

"Marry me."

Anders Kent wanted to take the words back the minute they'd left his mouth.

Marry me.

What had he been thinking? He'd just proposed to a complete and total stranger in a sterile room that smelled like soap and puppy chow. A stranger who was *dressed as a reindeer.* And now she was looking at him as if he was the crazy one.

Oh, the irony.

He wasn't crazy. Nor was he impulsive, all evidence to the contrary. He was simply desperate. Which was also ironic, considering Anders's name popped up in the tabloids from time to time as one of New York's most sought-after bachelors. Anders Kent had an office with a corner window in Wall Street's premier investment banking firm and a penthouse overlooking Central Park West. If he wanted something, he generally found a way to get it. Romantic entanglements included.

But his current predicament didn't have anything to do with romance. Far from it. There wasn't anything remotely romantic about sitting across a desk from your attorney and being told you had thirty days to find a wife.

Anders had been given just such an ultimatum at nine o'clock this morning, and his head had been spinning ever since.

Marriage?

No.

Hell no.

Anders didn't want to get married—to *anyone*, least of all the hostile woman beside him who looked as if she was on the verge of prying Lolly's puppy right out of his arms.

"What did you just say?" She swallowed, and the jingle bells at her throat did a little dance.

"Nothing." Anders shook his head. He sure as hell wasn't going to repeat himself. He shouldn't have opened his mouth to begin with.

You don't even know this woman's name.

His gut churned. In the brief span of time since he'd left his lawyer's office, something strange had happened to Anders. He'd begun to weigh every woman he came across as a potential wife…as if he truly had any intention to go through with the insane requirement.

He wouldn't. Couldn't. He'd fight it. He'd throw every dollar he had at fighting it until he won.

But legal battles took time. More often than not, they took years. And Anders didn't have years. He had a month.

"It didn't sound like nothing. It definitely sounded like a big fat *something*." The woman's eyes grew wide, panicked.

She'd gotten his message, loud and clear.

He should have phrased it differently, though. He was proposing a business arrangement, not an actual marriage.

Yes, he needed a wife. But not a real one, just a stand-in. A temporary wife. After Lolly's guardianship was properly settled, everything could go back to normal.

His chest tightened. *Normal* was a pipe dream. It didn't exist anymore. His life wouldn't be normal ever again.

He took a tense inhalation and looked away from the dancing reindeer. "Never mind."

"Never mind?" She threw her arms in the air. *Jingle, jingle, jingle.* "You can't just ask someone to marry you and then take it back. This isn't the season finale of *The Bachelor*."

"I've never seen that show," he said woodenly.

He couldn't marry this woman. She watched garbage television. She was bubbly, brash and far too emotional. She was a bleeding heart who spent her free time visiting shelter dogs. Plus, she obviously despised him.

It would never work.

Unless…

He frowned.

Unless the fact that they were so clearly ill-suited for one another would be an advantage. He couldn't marry anyone he actually found attractive. That would be a recipe for disaster. And he definitely wasn't attracted to the reindeer.

He *shouldn't* be attracted to her, anyway.

A surge of something that felt far too much like desire flowed through his veins. What the hell was wrong with him?

"I'm not going to marry you for a puppy," she said hotly. She looked him up and down. "No matter how…nice…the two of you look together."

She swallowed and averted her gaze, giving Anders an unobstructed view of the graceful curve of her neck.

Definitely a dancer, he thought. Her posture, coupled with the way she moved, was undeniably balletic. Beautiful, even in that silly costume.

"I thought you said I didn't look like the Yorkie type," he said.

Her cheeks went pink, but before she could respond the door swung open and a no-nonsense-looking woman wearing a T-shirt with Adopt, Don't Shop printed across the front of it extended her hand.

"Hello, Miss Wilde. Mr. Kent. I'm the shelter manager." She looked back and forth between them. "I understand there's been a mistake."

Anders nodded and glanced at Rudolph—whose actual name was Miss Wilde, apparently—and braced himself for the tirade that was sure to come. She hadn't let the adoption counselor get a word in edgewise. Why would she hold her tongue now?

But she didn't say a thing. Instead, she crossed her arms and stared daggers at him while the shelter manager reviewed their respective paperwork.

He'd dodged a bullet. There were countless single women in New York. He didn't know what had possessed him to propose to this one.

Still, there was a sadness in her eyes that made him feel like his heart was being squeezed in a vise. Anders had seen enough sadness in recent days that it made him want to do something to take away that melancholy look in her eyes—something that was sure to make her smile.

"Here," he said, holding the little dog toward her.

He had more than enough to worry about without adding alleged puppy thievery to the list. He'd simply have to find another dog for Lolly. It was sure to be easier than finding a wife.

"She's yours."

Chapter Two

The tiny dog squirmed in Chloe's arms as she watched the brooding man—her erstwhile fiancé—cross the length of the lobby and walk out the door in just three bold strides.

What just happened?

Wordlessly, she stared after him until the shelter manager cleared her throat.

"Well," she said. "I guess that settles that. The dog is yours if you still want her."

Chloe snapped back to the matter at hand. "I do. Definitely."

Of course she still wanted the puppy. She was just having a hard time switching gears from being proposed to by a total stranger to once again thinking about the logistics of puppy ownership.

"That was weird, though, wasn't it?" Chloe held the dog closer to her chest. The tiny animal smelled like shampoo and puppy breath, which was a comforting and welcome switch from the gritty aroma of Times Square. "Don't you think so?"

"Um." The shelter manager's smile faded. "I really couldn't say."

"That's right. You missed the crazy part." The puppy started gnawing on Chloe's thumb. Somewhere in her purse, she had a chew toy she'd purchased for a moment like this one, but she was too rattled to look for it. "He asked me to *marry* him."

The shelter manager gave a little start. "Oh, I didn't realize you and Mr. Kent knew each other."

Kent.

So that was his name. It swirled through her thoughts like a snowflake until she found herself combining it with hers.

Chloe Kent.

Mrs. Chloe Kent.

Her face went hot. "We don't. I've never seen him before in my life."

"Oh."

Chloe sneaked a glance at his paperwork, still sitting on the counter where he'd left it. "Anders Kent" was printed neatly in the name box.

"He just upped and asked me to marry him, and then he took it back." Chloe huffed out a sigh.

Of course this would happen to her. The hits just kept on coming. Instead of getting a normal proposal from a normal man—her ex, Steven, for instance—she got one from a total crackpot who promptly changed his mind.

Except he hadn't seemed like a crackpot. He actually seemed sort of charming, especially when he was holding the puppy. But come on, what handsome man didn't seem charming with a cute dog in his arms?

"Not that I considered it for even a second. It seems exceedingly rude to withdraw a proposal, though. I'm just saying." The puppy started to whine in her arms, so she bounced up and down a bit. *Jingle, jingle, jingle.* "Surely you agree."

The shelter manager sighed. "Honestly, as long as the puppy goes to a good home, I don't really care."

"Right. Of course." Why was she telling this woman about her almost-engagement to a perfect stranger?

More specifically, why couldn't she let the stunning incident go? She shouldn't be dwelling on it. It was a *non*-incident, as evidenced by the mysterious Anders Kent's speedy retraction, followed by his hasty exit.

"Do you want the dog or not?" The exasperated woman slid a paper across the counter toward Chloe.

"Absolutely." She scrawled her name on the designated line.

After all, she was here to adopt a puppy, not to get engaged.

Not now.

Not ever.

"Mr. Kent." Edith Summers, Anders's personal assistant, stood as he strode into the paneled entryway to his office. "We weren't expecting you to come in today."

Anders paused and nodded graciously at the older woman. He wasn't typically one for small talk in the workplace, but he hadn't seen Mrs. Summers since the funeral and her presence at that ghastly affair had been more comforting than he'd expected. Burying his brother and sister-in-law was by no means easy, but seeing his assistant sitting in the second pew, wearing her customary pearls and stoic, maternal expression, had made him feel a little less alone. A little less untethered.

"I changed my mind." Anders smiled stiffly.

He should say something. He should thank her, or at the very minimum, acknowledge her presence on that darkest of days. But just over Mrs. Summers's shoulder, Anders spotted his brother's name on the smooth oak door to the office next to his own, and the words died on his tongue.

Mrs. Summers followed his gaze, then squared her shoulders and cleared her throat. She'd been Anders's assistant long enough to know that what he needed now was normalcy. And normalcy meant work. It meant numbers and spreadsheets and meetings with investors. It meant being at his desk from sunup to sundown…

But that would have to change now, wouldn't it?

"Very well. I'll get you a cup of coffee and then we can go over your schedule," Mrs. Summers said.

"Thank you." He held her gaze long enough to impart all the things he couldn't say—thank you for being there, thank you for not trying to make him talk about his feelings or force him to go home. The list was long.

"Of course." Her eyes flashed with sympathy, and Anders's chest wound itself into a hard, suffocating tangle as she bustled past him toward the executive break room.

How long would it be this way?

How long would it be before he could stand in this place where he once felt so capable, so impenetrable, and not feel like his heart had just been put through a paper shredder?

Months. Years, maybe.

Lolly's sweet, innocent face rose to the forefront of his consciousness, and he knew with excruciating clarity that no amount of time would be sufficient. He'd feel this way for a lifetime. He'd carry the loss to his grave.

But he couldn't think about that now. Lolly was depending on him. His niece was only five years old, too young to grasp the permanence of what had just happened to her…what had happened to them both. Anders, on the other hand, was all too aware.

He was even more aware of feeling that he wasn't quite up to the task of raising a child. Anders didn't know the first thing about being a father. Not that he would ever come close to replacing Grant and Olivia in Lolly's life. But having lost his own parents at an early age, he knew that children as young as his niece didn't understand words like *guardian* and *custody*. Even if Lolly continued calling him Uncle Anders, he'd become so much more than that. He'd be the one to teach her how to ride a bicycle and help her with her homework. He'd be the one cheering at her high school graduation and pulling his hair out when she learned how to drive. He'd be the one to walk her down the aisle at her wedding.

For all practical purposes, he'd be her father. He'd spend the rest of his life walking in his younger brother's shoes.

If he was lucky.

"Shall I set up a meeting between you and the estate lawyer?" Mrs. Summers placed a double cappuccino with perfect foam on the desk in front of Anders and took a seat in one of the leather wingback guest chairs facing him. As usual, she held the tablet she used to keep track of his calendar in one hand and a pair of reading glasses in the other.

"Already done. I saw him this morning." Anders stared into his coffee. It was going to take a lot more than caffeine to get him through the next few weeks.

"Oh." His secretary blinked. "Everything all right, then?"

Anders took a deep breath and considered how much, exactly, he should share with his secretary. On one hand, she was his employee. On the other, she might be the closest thing he had to a friend now that his brother—who also happened to be his business partner—was gone. Such was the life of a workaholic.

"Not really," he said quietly.

The phone on Mrs. Summers's desk began to ring,

but when she popped out of her chair to go answer it, Anders motioned for her to stay put.

"Leave it. Just let it roll to voice mail." He took a sip of his cappuccino. She'd gone easy on the foam this time, and it slid down his throat, hot and bitter. Just like his mood.

Mrs. Summers frowned. "You're beginning to worry me, Mr. Kent. Is something wrong?"

Nothing that a wife wouldn't fix.

He closed his eyes and saw the puzzled face of the woman from the animal shelter—her wide brown eyes and lush pink lips, arranged in a perfect O of surprise.

Marry me.

God, he'd actually said that, hadn't he? The past week had been rough, no doubt about it. It was astounding how much a single phone call could change things, could eviscerate your life so cleanly as if it were a blade of some sort. A knife to the gut.

But until this morning, Anders had been hanging on. He'd had to, for Lolly's sake and for the sake of the business. Grief was a luxury he couldn't afford. Not now, not yet. Besides, if he let himself bend beneath the crushing weight of loss, he wouldn't be able to get back up—not after the things he'd said to Grant the night before the accident.

Anders and his brother rarely argued, and when they did, it was typically about the business. As two of the name partners in one of the most influential investment banking firms on Wall Street, they always had one another's back, but that didn't mean blind support. They challenged each other. They made each other better.

Their last argument had been different, though. Anders had gone too far—he'd made it personal. There'd been raised voices and slammed doors, and then nothing but an uncomfortable silence after Grant stormed out of the building. It had been their most heated exchange to date, but that was okay. They were brothers, for crying out loud. Grant would get over it.

But he couldn't get over it, because now he was gone. And Anders couldn't even bring himself to set foot in his dead brother's empty office.

It was easier to stay on this side of that closed door. Safer.

Anders had managed to push their final confrontation into the darkest corner of his consciousness that he could find, and at first, it had been remarkably easy. He'd had a funeral to plan and Grant's in-laws to deal with and a new, tiny person sleeping in his penthouse.

He was beginning to crack now. That much was obvious. Tiny fissures were forming in the carefully constructed wall he'd managed to build around the memory of his last conversation with Grant. Any minute now, it would all come flooding back. The effort to keep it at bay was crippling, as evidenced by his spontaneous marriage proposal to a woman dressed in a reindeer costume.

"There are some issues with Lolly's guardianship." Anders swallowed. The knot that had formed in his throat during the funeral service was still sitting like a stone.

Mrs. Summers shook her head. "I don't understand. You're her godfather."

"Yes, I am." He'd dutifully attended the church service at St. Patrick's Cathedral and poured water over Lolly's fragile newborn head. It had been a done deal.

Or so he'd thought.

He took another scalding gulp of his cappuccino. Then he set the china cup back down on the desk with enough force that liquid sloshed over the rim. "As it turns out, the legalities of the matter are a bit more complicated."

"How so?"

"When Grant and Olivia drafted their wills, they made my guardianship of Lolly conditional. The only way I can be awarded full custody is if I'm married."

The tablet slid out of Mrs. Summers's hand and fell to the floor with a clunk. She didn't bother picking it up. "Married?"

"Married." He nodded. Maybe if they both kept repeating the word, the reality of his situation would sink in.

"But..." The older woman's voice drifted off, which was probably for the best. Anders could only imagine the trajectory of her thoughts.

But you haven't been on more than three dates with the same woman in years.

But you're a workaholic.

And to quote his brother...

But you're dead inside.

"Exactly," Anders said, because it didn't really matter which objection caused her hesitation. They all fit.

"So that's it, then? What happens to Lolly?"

"Lolly's staying put." They'd take her away over his dead body. He'd made a promise to his brother that rainy day in St. Patrick's Cathedral, and he intended to keep it. He owed Grant that much. It was the least he could do. "I just have to find a wife."

The shocked expression on Mrs. Summers's face gave way to one of perplexed amusement. "Find a wife? It's as simple as that, is it?"

"Yes." He gave her a curt nod.

Simple was a necessity.

Frankly, the more Anders thought about it, the more he liked the idea of an arranged marriage. A temporary wife was exactly what he needed. He'd handle it like a basic merger. After all, those were his specialty. No messy emotions, no expectations—just a simple business transaction between two consenting adults.

Two consenting adults who wouldn't sleep together or have any other sort of romantic entanglement.

Maybe I really am dead inside.

Fine. So be it.

Maybe Grant had hit the nail on the head when he'd made that astute accusation right before he turned on his heel and stormed out of the office five days ago. Anders hoped he had. He'd love nothing more than to remain in his current state of numbness for the rest of his godforsaken life.

"My husband and I only knew each other for six months before we got married, and he was the love of my life." Mrs. Summers gave Anders a watery smile. "You're absolutely right. It doesn't have to be complicated."

Anders swallowed around the rock in his throat. "I don't have six months. I have until Christmas."

She gaped at him, and he took advantage of her silence to abruptly fill her in on the rest of it. Having this conversation was more humbling than he'd anticipated. "If I'm not married by the end of the calendar year, Lolly goes to the alternate guardians—Olivia's sister and her husband. Lolly can't go to them. They live in Kansas, and her entire life would be upended. Plus, they've already got five kids of their own, and while I'm sure they're competent parents, they weren't my brother's first choice."

Nor was Anders, technically. Grant and Olivia wanted Lolly raised by Anders *plus one*, as if the matter of guardianship could be worded like a wedding invitation.

Was it even legal? Possibly, according to his lawyer. But they didn't have time to battle it out in court.

Even if they had, Anders would have had to speculate in front of a judge and jury why his own brother would place such a condition on his role in Lolly's life in the event she became orphaned. He would be forced to admit that the provision in the will had taken him by surprise, but he knew precisely why it was there.

If Grant and Olivia couldn't be there for Lolly,

they wanted her to grow up in a nuclear family—a home with a mom and dad. But that wasn't the only reason. They knew that Anders loved their daughter, but they also knew he couldn't be trusted to get up and walk away from Wall Street at a reasonable hour every day. Work was his first love, his only love. And that wasn't good enough for Lolly.

Hell, even Anders knew it wasn't.

He would change. Had they really thought he wouldn't? He'd turn his life inside out and upside down for that little girl.

Yet here you sit.

The paneled walls of his office felt as if they were closing in around him. Anders fixated on the smooth surface of his desk and breathing in and out until the feeling passed.

When at last he looked up, the tablet was back in Mrs. Summers's hands again and her glasses were perched on the end of her nose.

"Tell me how I can help," she said.

A fleeting sense of relief passed through him. Help was precisely what he needed, and Mrs. Summers was efficient beyond measure. He could do this. He had to. "Get me the names and contact information for every woman I've dated in the past twelve months."

"Yes, sir." She jotted something down with her stylus.

"Better make that the past eighteen months, just to be safe." He took a deep inhalation. It felt good to have a plan, even if said plan was a long shot. Reaching out to old girlfriends made more sense than proposing to strangers.

"If I might make a suggestion, sir. Perhaps you should consider..." Mrs. Summers tipped her head in the direction of the office across the hall from Anders's, which belonged to another partner in the firm—Penelope Reed.

Anders grew still. He hadn't realized anyone in the office knew about the arrangement he had with Penelope. So much for subtlety.

"No." He shook his head.

It wasn't completely out of the question, but Penelope was his last resort. True, they occasionally shared a bed. And true, their relationship was strings-free, as businesslike as a coupling could possibly be.

But marrying someone within the firm was a terrible idea. They could hide the occasional one-night stand, but a marriage was another matter entirely.

"Very well." Mrs. Summers nodded. "It was just an idea."

"I'll keep it in mind." He shifted uncomfortably in his chair and wondered what it meant that he'd felt more comfortable proposing to a stranger than to a woman he bedded from time to time. Nothing good, that was for sure. "In the meantime, I also need to find another puppy."

Mrs. Summers peered at him over the top of her glasses. "Did you miss your appointment at the animal shelter this afternoon? I thought I'd programmed it into your BlackBerry."

"No, I was there. But the shelter made some kind of

mistake. They promised the dog to someone else." For a brief, blissful moment, Anders's attention strayed from his messy life, and he thought about the graceful woman in the reindeer costume—her soulful eyes, holly berry lips and perfect, impertinent mouth. Somewhere in the back of his head, he could have sworn he heard jingle bells.

"What a shame. Lolly would have loved that little dog." His assistant pressed a hand to her heart.

Anders had screwed up a lot of things lately. His list of mistakes was longer than the line to take pictures with Santa at Macy's, but he had a feeling he'd done the right thing when he'd walked away from the animal shelter empty-handed. Maybe he wasn't as big of a Scrooge as everyone thought he was.

Dead inside.

A headache bloomed at the back of Anders's skull. "There are other puppies. I suspect it worked out for the best."

Mrs. Summers narrowed her gaze, studied him for a beat and then nodded. "Things usually do."

Did they?

God, he hoped so.

"I think I'm going to take the rest of the afternoon off, after all." He stood, buttoned his suit jacket and shifted his weight from one foot to the other.

This office was his sanctuary. He'd always felt more at home at his desk, glued to the market's highs and lows, than he did at his luxury penthouse with its sweeping views of Central Park and the Natural History Museum. But today it felt different, strange…

He wondered if it would ever feel like home again, and if it didn't, where he was supposed to find peace.

"Call the nanny and tell her I'm on the way to fetch Lolly." Maybe he'd take her to see the tree at Rockefeller Center or for a carriage ride through the park. Something Christmassy.

Like the Rockettes show at Radio City Music Hall?

His jaw clenched tight.

"Yes, Mr. Kent. And I'll look into the puppy situation and send you a list of available dogs that might be a good fit." Mrs. Summers looked up from her tablet. "Would you like me to try and find another Yorkie mix?"

He heard the woman's voice again—so confident, so cynical in her assessment of his character.

You really don't seem like the Yorkie type.

What did that even mean?

Did she picture him with something less fluffy and adorable, like a bulldog? Or a snake? More to the point, why had that assumption stuck with him and rubbed him so entirely the wrong way?

"Anything. I'm open to suggestions," he muttered. Then on second thought, he said, "Scratch that. I want a lapdog—something cute and affectionate, on the smaller side. A real cupcake of a dog."

Mrs. Summers stifled a smile. "Of course, sir."

"The sweeter, the better."

Chapter Three

The afternoon following Chloe's odd encounter at the animal shelter, she tucked her new puppy into a playpen containing the candy cane–striped dog bed and a dozen or so new toys and then trudged her way through the snow-covered West Village to the Wilde School of Dance.

It was time to face the music.

She couldn't keep lying to her family about her job. Just this morning, she'd thought she spotted her cousin Ryan walking through Times Square while she'd been on flyer duty. She'd ducked behind one of the area's ubiquitous costumed characters—a minion in a Santa hat—but there was no hiding her blinking antlers.

Luckily, the man in the slim tailored suit hadn't

been her cousin. Nor had it been her brother, Zander. To her immense relief, she also ruled out the possibility that he was the man who'd proposed to her yesterday—Anders Kent. This guy's shoulders weren't quite as broad, and the cut of his jaw was all wrong. His posture was far too laid-back and casual. He seemed like a regular person out for a stroll on his lunch break, whereas Anders had been brimming with intensity, much like the city itself—gritty and glamorous. So beautifully electric.

Not that she'd been thinking about him for the duration of her two-hour shift. She quite purposefully *hadn't*. But being on flyer duty was such a mindless job, and while she flashed her Rockette smile for the tourists and ground her teeth against the wind as it swept between the skyscrapers, he kept sneaking back into her consciousness. The harder she tried not to think about him, the clearer the memory of their interaction became, until it spun through her mind on constant repeat, like a favorite holiday movie. *Love Actually* or *It's a Wonderful Life*.

Chloe huffed out a sigh. If life was even remotely wonderful, she wouldn't be so hung up on a meaningless encounter with a stranger. Which was precisely why she had to stop pretending everything was fine and come to terms with reality. She was no longer a professional dancer. She might never perform that loathsome toy soldier routine again, and if she didn't humble herself and come clean with the rest of the Wildes, they were sure to find out some other way and her embarrassment would be multiplied tenfold. Emily Wilde was practically omniscient. It was a miracle Chloe's mother hadn't busted her already.

Sure enough, the minute Chloe pushed through the door of the Wilde School of Dance, she could feel Emily's eyes on her from clear across the room. Her mother was deep in conversation with a slim girl in a black leotard—one of her ballet students, no doubt—but her penetrating gaze was trained on Chloe.

Here we go.

Chloe smiled and attempted a flippy little wave, as if this was any ordinary day and she stopped by the studio all the time. She didn't, of course, making this whole situation more awkward and humbling than she could bear.

When was the last time she'd set foot inside this place? A while—even longer than she'd realized. She didn't recognize half the faces in the recital photographs hanging on the lobby walls, and the smooth maple floors had taken quite a beating since she'd twirled across them in pointe shoes as a teenager. The sofa in the parents' waiting area had a definite sag in its center that hadn't been there when Chloe spent hours sprawled across it doing her homework after school.

Was her mother still using the same blue record player and worn practice albums instead of a digital sound system? Yes, apparently. The turntable sat perched on a shelf in the corner of the main classroom, right where it had been since before Chloe was born.

At least Emily was no longer teaching back-to-back classes all day, every day. Chloe's sister-in-law, Allegra, had taken over the majority of the curriculum. From the looks of things, Allegra's intermediate ballet class had just ended. She waved at Chloe from behind the classroom's big picture window as happy ten- and eleven-year-olds in pink tights and soft ballet slippers spilled out of the studio, weaving around Chloe with girlish, balletic grace.

Her throat grew tight as a wave of nostalgia washed over her. Everything was all so different, and yet still exactly the same as she remembered.

She'd grown up here. In total, she'd probably spent more time between these faded blue walls than she had in the grand family brownstone on Riverside Drive. If family lore was to be believed, she'd taken her first steps in her mother's office between boxes of tap shoes and recital costumes. Just months afterward, she'd learned to plié at the barre in the classroom with the old blue record player.

Chloe's first kiss had happened here, too—with a boy from the School of American Ballet Theatre during rehearsals for *Romeo and Juliet*. It had been a stage kiss, but her heart beat as wildly as hummingbird wings, and when the boy's lips first touched hers, she'd forgotten about pointed toes and the blister on her heel from her new pointe shoes.

The kiss might have been fake, but the warmth of his lips was real, as was the feeling that this school, this place that she knew so well, was etched permanently on her soul. She'd always come back here. It was her home.

I should have come back sooner.

She'd meant to. But somehow days turned into weeks and weeks turned into months, and then her father died. Walking in her childhood footsteps after his heart attack was just too painful, so she'd taken the easy way out and stayed away. She'd thrown herself fully into the Rockettes and, like everything in her life, the family dance school took a back seat to her career.

And now here she was—jobless, with no close friends, superficial relationships with her family members and no love life whatsoever now that Steven had so unceremoniously dumped her after the Thanksgiving parade mishap.

Perfect. She'd somehow become the horrible character in a Christmas movie who required divine intervention to become a decent person again. Except there wasn't an angel in sight, was there?

Again, Anders Kent's chiseled features flashed in her mind. She blinked. Hard.

"Chloe!" Allegra clicked the classroom door shut behind her and pulled Chloe into a hug. "What a wonderful surprise. What are you doing here? Isn't this your busy season? Aren't you performing ten times a day or something crazy like that?"

Before she could form a response, the teen ballerina bade Emily goodbye. Chloe stepped out of the hug and held her breath as her mother approached.

"Hello, dear. Isn't this a lovely surprise." Emily kissed her cheek, but the warm greeting didn't alleviate her sense of shame.

If anything, it made her feel worse.

"Hi, Mom. Allegra. It's great to see you both." Chloe could feel her smile start to tremble.

Don't cry. The only thing that could make her confession more painful was if she fell apart before she could get the words out.

"Are you okay, dear?" Emily glanced at the dainty antique watch strapped around her wrist. She'd been wearing it as long as Chloe could remember. "It's the middle of the day. Shouldn't you be performing in the matinee?"

This was it. This was the moment to spill the beans and admit she was the Rockette who'd become YouTube famous for ruining the Thanksgiving Day parade.

She took a deep breath. "No, I'm actually not performing anymore. For now, anyway."

"What do you mean, you're not performing?" Emily's face fell.

The disappointment in her eyes was a knife to Chloe's heart. For all Chloe's mistakes, Emily had always been her biggest supporter. Chloe had missed months' worth of family dinners and get-togethers, but when it came to performing, she'd never failed to make her dancer mother proud. Until now.

"I'm on hiatus for a while." She swallowed and shifted her gaze over Emily's shoulder so she wouldn't have to see her mother's crushed expression, but then she found herself staring at a slick, glossy poster from one of her own Christmas shows.

The poster hung in a frame surrounded by photographs of herself in various Rockette costumes. The arrangement was practically a shrine.

"Oh dear, you're not injured, are you?" Emily's hand fluttered to her heart.

"Please don't worry, Mom. I'm fine." *I'm just a world-class coward.* She couldn't do it. She couldn't confess to being fired, not while she was standing there, facing the Chloe wall of fame.

Besides, her mom had just given her an excellent idea. An injury, even a small one, would buy her some time to make things right. She could start helping out at the school. She'd answer the phones, manage the dance moms—anything—and once she'd proved her devotion to her family again, she'd finally tell them everything.

Because she was definitely telling the truth, 100 percent. She was just delaying it a tiny bit longer.

Seriously? Just fess up already.

"It's only a sprain," she heard herself say, and immediately wished the floor would open up and swallow her whole.

Allegra gasped. "Oh, no. Please say it's not your ankle."

Chloe looked down at her feet. She'd worn Uggs, because it was freezing out, but if she'd had an injured ankle, it would be wrapped. She might even be on crutches. "Um, no. It's my calf."

"Your calf?" Emily lifted a brow.

"Yes. There's a terrible knot in it." Could she have come up with a more ridiculous lie? There was no way her mother was buying this.

"I see," Emily said quietly…so quietly that Chloe had the distinct impression that her mother really did understand what was happening, but was so unable to face the truth of the situation that she couldn't even say it out loud.

But if Emily sensed Chloe was being less than truthful, she didn't admit it.

"That's a shame, sweetheart. But whatever circumstances brought you back, I'm glad you're here." She smiled. "Really glad."

Chloe took a deep breath. "Me, too. I was actually hoping you could put me to work."

"Here at the studio?" Allegra said.

"Yes. I'd love to help run things around here with the two of you. I'll do whatever you need."

"But your calf…" Allegra's gaze drifted downward.

"She's right," Emily chimed in. "Your calf could get in the way of doing any teaching. Plus, I'm afraid we can't really afford it."

The school was having money troubles? No wonder things looked a little worse for wear. "I didn't realize…"

Of course she didn't. Maybe if she'd bothered to show up every now and then, she'd know what was going on.

"I think I might have an idea, but it would only be part-time," Emily said.

"That's okay." She needed a few hours a week off for flyer duty, anyway. "I'll do anything."

"We're doing *Baby Nutcracker* this year, and you'd be a perfect director."

"Baby Nutcracker?" Chloe had no idea what that meant, but she didn't ask. Whatever it was must have been added to the school's annual repertoire, and she didn't want to draw yet more attention to her prolonged absence. "That sounds like fun. I'd love to."

Emily and Allegra exchanged a glance.

"Are you sure? It might be part-time, but it's not an easy job," Allegra said.

"And you'd need to be around until Christmas Eve." Emily raised her brows, waiting for an answer.

Perfect. "I'm sure."

"Great. You can start right now." Emily brushed past her and held the door open for the crowd of parents with small children who'd appeared out of nowhere and were lined up on the sidewalk outside.

Wait. *What?*

"Now?" Chloe gulped.

"Now." Emily nodded.

Allegra leaned closer. "I'll help. You have no idea what you've gotten yourself into, do you?"

Thank God for sisters-in-law. "I'm clueless."

"*Baby Nutcracker* is a Christmas recital for the preballet students, aged three to five." She pushed open the door to the main classroom and waved Chloe inside. "It's an abbreviated version of the traditional *Nutcracker* ballet—same music, same characters, just a bit shorter."

Preschoolers dressed as mice, nutcrackers and a

sugarplum fairy? Yes, please. Who would turn down this job? "That sounds adorable."

Allegra crossed her arms. She seemed to be biting back a smirk. "When was the last time you taught preballet?"

Was this a trick question? "Never. I might have helped out back when I was a teenager, but that's the extent of my teaching experience."

Chloe slipped out of her coat. Luckily, she'd worn a black wraparound sweater and yoga pants—clothes she could move in.

"You can borrow these." Allegra tossed her a pair of ballet shoes. "If you think your calf will be okay."

"Thanks." She swallowed and slipped the shoes on. "I'm excited. This should be fun."

"The little ones are precious, and the production is definitely adorable. But they're a handful." She glanced over Chloe's shoulder. "And they're here."

Right. She could do this. She was usually onstage for a minimum of three shows a day for the entire month of December. Putting together a half-hour ballet recital for a few preschoolers would probably be easy by comparison.

You wanted to be involved, and now you are.

She took a deep breath and turned, following Allegra's gaze toward the picture window that overlooked the lobby. The space was suddenly packed with strollers and tiny bodies dressed in candy-colored ballet clothes. It looked like every mom in the Village had turned up with a toddler in tow.

How could they possibly have money problems?

Enrollment seemed to be booming. "Allegra, how bad is the school struggling?"

"Pretty bad." Allegra sighed. "We had the big dance-athon fund-raiser a while back, so the business is out of the red. But we're still barely getting by. We've got just enough to pay the bills every month. I keep thinking that if we could give the studio a major face-lift, we could attract serious dance students. Maybe we could even hold a summer intensive for one of the dance companies."

"That's a great idea." But it would never happen in the school's current condition.

Chloe looked around again, and her gaze snagged on all the little things that needed to be fixed—the cracked walls, the scuffed floors, the faded furniture. Even the window overlooking the lobby had a tiny spiderweb of cracks in the corner. She frowned at it, until something beyond the glass caught her attention.

Correction: not something. Some*one*.

His head towered above the crowd, and his expression was as grim and intense as ever. Chloe had never seen anyone look so woefully out of place at a ballet studio before. It would have been comical if the sight of him hadn't been such a shock.

"Brace yourself. I'm going to open the door and let the kids inside." Allegra paused midway across the room. "Are you okay? You look like you've seen a ghost."

Not a ghost. A thief.

A *puppy* thief.

The man on the other side of the window finally

glanced her way. He did a double take, and then his gaze collided with hers.

She forgot how to breathe for a second. All day long she'd kept imagining that she'd seen him, and now here he was in the flesh, as if she'd somehow conjured him.

Anders Kent.

Her would-be fiancé.

Chapter Four

Anders went still as their gazes locked through the picture window. Around him, chaos reigned as a dozen mothers wrestled their children out of snow boots and into pale pink ballet shoes and tutus. The floor was littered with coats, stray mittens and far more strollers than could safely fit into the small space. But he forgot all of it the moment he spotted the dancer on the other side of the glass.

Her.

She was dressed normally this time—no reindeer suit in sight—but he recognized her instantly. She had that same unforgettable graceful neck, same supple spine, same holly berry lips. Tiny earrings shaped liked candy canes dangled from her ears, brushing lightly against her skin in a way that made Anders forget he was standing in the middle of mommy-and-me chaos. He could only stand and stare, with all his attention focused on that swan-like curve, wondering what her body would feel like in his hands. Soft…warm.

His fingers balled into fists at his sides, and then she waved, snapping him out of his trance. He lifted an eyebrow in acknowledgment.

Definitely the same woman, in all her Christmas-loving glory.

"Can we go in now?" Lolly tugged at his pant leg.

He looked down at her tiny feet, trying to figure out if he'd gotten her ballet shoes on the correct ones. He still wasn't certain. She seemed somewhat happy, though, and that was all that mattered. "Sure, pumpkin."

Most of the other kids charged into the classroom on their own, but Lolly wanted an escort. The morning after the accident, when Anders told her that her mommy and daddy were in heaven now and wouldn't be coming home, she'd clung to him and soaked his shirt with tears.

She'd been more like her usual chatty self in the past few days, but still had moments when she wanted to hold his hand, or be carried so that she could wrap her tiny arms around his neck. Anders had a feeling she just needed to know he wasn't going to disappear.

He wouldn't.

Not if he could help it.

Lolly led him into the classroom, but the minute they crossed the threshold, she dropped his hand to join her friends, sitting cross-legged in a cluster of frothy pink tulle in front of the large mirrored wall.

He lingered for a moment, hesitant to leave her there. And maybe a part of him—some shadow of his former self that remembered what it was like to wish for something, to want—didn't want to walk away from Miss Wilde again.

What are you doing? He had a mountain of tasks to accomplish today, starting with finding a way to convince Penelope Reed to marry him. He'd thought about the matter long and hard, and realistically, she was his only option.

He turned to go, but before he could take a step, the whimsical Miss Wilde tapped him on the shoulder.

"Going somewhere?" she said.

A smile tugged at his lips as he spun to face her. He barely recognized the sensation. It felt like years since he'd smiled. "Yes. Back to the office."

"I'm Chloe, by the way. We didn't get as far as names yesterday. Parents are welcome to stay and watch." Her soft brown eyes seemed almost hopeful.

He shook his head. "I can't. I..." *I've got to go get engaged.*

"Hello, Mr. Kent." Allegra, the dance teacher he'd met at Lolly's last recital, paused to stand beside Chloe. She glanced back and forth between them. "You two know each other?"

"No," said Anders, at the exact moment Chloe Wilde contradicted him by nodding and saying yes.

Then she frowned and glared at him in much the same way she had the day before when she'd accused him of being a puppy thief. "Seriously? You asked me to marry you yesterday and now you're pretending we don't know each other?"

Allegra coughed—loudly—but Anders's gaze remained glued to Chloe. "You're not going to let that go, are you?"

She smiled at him, and the curve of her red lips was far too sweet. Visions of sugarplums danced in his head. "Nope."

"Wait—I'm confused." Allegra frowned. "What happened to Steven?"

"Who's Steven?" he asked, before he could stop himself.

Chloe's cheeks flared a lovely shade of pink. "He's no one."

Anders glanced at Allegra for confirmation, although why he cared about a person he'd never heard of before was a mystery.

Sure it is. You know *why.*

Allegra bit her lip and then caved under his gaze. "He's not exactly no one. Chloe, didn't you and Steven date for nearly three years?"

Something hardened in Anders's gut, and if he didn't know better, he would have recognized the feeling as jealousy.

Impossible. He didn't even know this woman. He'd laid eyes on her exactly twice, and both times he'd found her borderline annoying. Attractive, sure—he wasn't blind, after all. But he didn't typically go for the adorably quirky type, and if Chloe was anything, she was that. Compared to most women he dated, she was sort of a mess.

Then again, it wasn't as if those women were lining up to marry him. He'd spent the previous evening getting back in touch with his dates from the past few months, and at first, most of them had been happy to hear from him. But as soon as he'd brought up the whole marriage-of-convenience idea, their enthusiasm waned. He'd been hung up on more times than he could count.

Chloe squared her slender shoulders and gave her chin a defiant lift. "Steven and I broke up. It wasn't working out and we agreed to go our separate ways. No big deal."

Wrong. The flash of pain in Chloe's soft doe eyes told him it was a very big deal, but he didn't press for an explanation. He wasn't altogether sure why he was even still standing there.

"Wow, I had no idea. I'm so sorry. I don't really know what to say." Allegra's gaze flicked toward him again.

He held up his hands. "I had nothing to do with it."

How was this his life? He should be facilitating an acquisition right now, or better yet, proposing to Penelope Reed, instead of standing in a ballet school wondering why the enigmatic Chloe Wilde was suddenly single.

"I should go," he blurted.

Penelope was the logical choice, in spite of their working relationship. She was reliable and discreet. He knew precisely what he'd be getting into if she agreed to a business marriage with him. It would be clean, simple and orderly, which was precisely the sort of relationship he needed right now, even if it was temporary.

As if on cue, Lolly appeared. She'd broken away from the group of little girls sitting cross-legged in front of the mirror and was now standing at his feet with her arms wrapped around his shins.

Too soon.

He shouldn't have brought her here. She'd been doing so well, and she'd been asking about going back to dance class, so he'd consulted his late brother's calendar and figured out Lolly's schedule. For a five-year-old, she was fiercely independent, brimming with confidence. Anders chalked it up to her Manhattan upbringing, but she was still just a child—a child who'd lost her mom and dad.

He should have waited another week or two. Better yet, he should have thrown that crazy schedule out the window and never come here.

But when Anders crouched down and peeled her slender arms from his legs, intent on scooping her up and walking out the door, she turned her back on him and gazed up at Chloe.

"Are you my teacher? I've never seen you here before," she said.

Chloe bent down so she was at eye level with Lolly. "I'm new." She pulled a face. "Sort of."

"Is that you on the picture outside?" Lolly pointed toward the lobby.

Of course Anders had noticed the framed poster

of Chloe in her flirty Santa costume and silver tap shoes, along with the multitude of surrounding photographs from her performances with the Rockettes. It would have been impossible not to. Even if he'd somehow missed it, Lolly's reaction would have clued him in.

She'd looked at the poster with stars in her eyes as they'd walked past, and she'd apparently just realized the beautiful dancer from the picture was here in the flesh, standing in the same room.

"That's me," Chloe said brightly.

"You look like a Christmas princess." Lolly tilted her head and looked Chloe up and down. "*Are* you a Christmas princess?"

And just like that, Anders was in over his head. He hadn't even formulated a Santa Claus plan yet, much less given any thought to princesses and fairy tales and storybook endings. How on earth was he going to raise a little girl?

Hell, maybe his brother had been right when he'd added the marriage clause to the guardianship paragraph in his will. Anders didn't know the first thing about being a dad.

"Not exactly," Chloe said. And before Lolly's face could fall, she added, "Christmas is a magical time, though. Just like a real-life fairy tale. And you know what? The ballet we're putting together for Christmas Eve has all sorts of wonderful parts—fairies, dancing snowflakes and even a few snow queens."

Lolly's eyes went as wide as saucers, and when her tiny mouth curved into a smile that lit up her whole face, some of the tightness in Anders's chest unraveled. After days of struggling to take a full inhalation, he could almost breathe again.

"Can I be a queen?" Lolly's quiet voice was as reverent as if she were speaking to Cinderella herself.

"We'll see. But no matter what, you'll get to dress up in a pretty costume and dance and twirl in front of an audience." Chloe glanced at Anders and gave him a quick wink. So quick he almost thought he'd imagined it. "Your daddy here might even bring you flowers."

And with those words, everything within him hardened again. They were a death blow. He couldn't breathe, couldn't speak, couldn't think. All he could do was stand there with his hands on Lolly's petite shoulders, choking on the truth while his ears roared.

Your daddy here...

Damn it.

Of course she'd assume he was Lolly's father. He should have seen it coming. Maybe he would have if he hadn't been so distracted by Chloe the Christmas Princess. And her perfectly bow-shaped, perfectly impertinent mouth.

He was mucking everything up.

Already.

"He's not my daddy," Lolly said, as casually as if she'd just announced the sky was blue.

"Oh." Chloe rested a hand on her chest, and for reasons he didn't want to contemplate, Anders's gaze darted to her unadorned ring finger. "I'm sorry. I thought..."

"He's my uncle." Lolly shrugged.

Anders gave her shoulders a gentle squeeze. "Why don't you go sit down, pumpkin? I think class is about to start."

"Okay." She threw her arms around him for a goodbye hug.

Anders bent low to hold her tight until she skipped back into place with the other children. When he straightened, he could see questions shining in Chloe's eyes—eyes that were the color of hot cocoa on frosty winter nights and seemed as if they could wrap around him like a blanket, enveloping him in warmth, making him feel at home.

Her lips parted, and he knew if he stayed, she'd ask about Lolly's mom and dad and he'd be forced to tell her everything, which was something he desperately didn't want to do. She'd been the first person in days who'd looked at him without a hint of pity in her gaze. He hadn't realized how much he'd needed a woman to look at him like that, but he had.

It made him feel human again. Like a man.

And it also made him wonder if he hadn't needed just any woman to see him as a man, but specifically *this* woman. If he'd been the type of person who believed in fairy tales, he might think that perhaps he'd been waiting for Chloe to prance into his life all along, reindeer suit and all.

But he wasn't.

Storybook endings were a fallacy. Anders had learned that lesson a hell of a long time ago, and now Lolly was learning it, too, in the most painful way possible. So once again, Anders turned his back on Chloe Wilde and left without so much as saying goodbye.

Chloe could barely concentrate as she ran the young children in her class through a simple round of pliés and tendus at the barre, followed by a giggly, boisterous round of chassés across the studio. For one thing, she couldn't believe the pitiful state of the wood floor beneath their tiny feet. A worn path extended from one corner of the room to the other, faded by decades of balletic turns and leaps.

Most dance schools didn't even have wood floors anymore. For years now, the trend had been performance floors—sheet vinyl laid over a sprung surface. Unlike wood, performance floors were slip resistant, resulting in fewer injuries and easier training for younger students. The elasticity absorbed shock and allowed dancers to leap higher. Emily should have replaced the floors years ago. No wonder enrollment was down.

But new floors cost thousands of dollars, and apparently money was more scarce around here than Chloe had realized. She wished she could do more to help.

She also wished she could stop thinking about Lolly Kent's handsome uncle. He'd been undeniably swoony at the animal shelter, holding the tiny puppy in his large, masculine hands. But seeing him with that precious little girl in his arms was almost more than Chloe could handle. It should be illegal for hot bachelors to walk around holding adorable children or tiny animals. Honestly.

His niece was a good dancer, too. She had great turnout for her age, but more important, she had charisma. Unlike technique, stage presence was something that couldn't be taught, and Lolly had it in spades. Chloe couldn't take her eyes off her, and it had nothing to do with Anders.

Not much, anyway.

It was only natural to be curious, though, wasn't it? And that was all she was experiencing—simple curiosity. Because it certainly wasn't attraction. She had far more important things to worry about at the moment than her nonexistent love life. Things like keeping track of all the lies she'd been telling lately. It was getting out of hand. If she didn't start telling the truth, she was going to need a spreadsheet to keep track of what came out of her mouth.

She had enough on her plate right now simply dealing with reviving her career, while at the same time doing something to alleviate all the guilt she felt about being the prodigal daughter. Also, as much as she hated to admit it, the breakup with Steven had gotten to her.

How could it not? Now that she was no longer performing, he thought she wasn't good enough. Deep down, she was starting to believe it, too. She'd devoted her whole life to dance. Without it, she wasn't sure who she was anymore.

Which was precisely why she had no interest in

dating—or marrying—Anders Kent. Not that he'd asked…again.

Still, when a nanny showed up to collect Lolly after class, Chloe's heart practically sank to her ballet slippers. The undeniable stab of disappointment she felt at the prospect of not seeing him again was confirmation enough to stay away from the man. Steven had been safe. They'd been good together, but not *too* good. She'd enjoyed spending time with him, but there'd been no goose bumps when he kissed her good-night. No butterflies swarming in her belly when she saw him across a crowded room. If her father's sudden heart attack had taught her anything, it was that life had a way of yanking the rug out from under you when you least expected it. She didn't want to fall madly in love with anyone. Falling in like was just fine. Safe. Which meant her relationship with Steven had been perfect, except now it was over. And now she also got the definite impression that Anders Kent was anything but safe.

There was something quite dangerous about his cool blue eyes and his perfect bone structure. His odd habit of doing or saying something nice when she least expected it was definitely alarming. When he'd handed her the puppy at the animal shelter and then walked out the door empty-handed, there'd been butterflies aplenty fluttering around her insides.

So really, it was best if she never set eyes on him again. And she probably wouldn't. Uncles didn't typically tote their nieces to and from ballet class.

Maybe she should ask, though, just to be sure. If

he was going to be coming to the studio on a regular basis, she needed to be prepared.

Purely so she could avoid him.

Obviously.

"Class went well, don't you think?" Chloe aimed a Windex bottle at the walled mirror, where sticky little handprints decorated the glass from barre-level down.

Allegra handed her a roll of paper towels. "It did. I knew you'd be great, but it never hurts to have reinforcements when so many small children are involved."

Chloe laughed. "You can say that again. At one point, I saw a little boy hanging upside down from the barre like a monkey."

"He sounds like a great candidate for the part of the mouse king. You can throw in some cute tumbling choreography. The parents will eat it up on performance night."

"So it's mostly family that comes to the performance? Moms and dads, sisters and brothers..." She scrubbed hard at an invisible spot on the mirror. "Uncles."

Allegra met her gaze in the reflection and lifted a brow. "Any particular uncle you have in mind?"

Was she that obvious?

Yes, apparently she was. "No."

Allegra snorted.

"Fine. Maybe." Chloe wadded up her paper towel and lobbed it at Allegra's head.

She caught it midair. "That's what I thought. Tell

me the truth—did Anders Kent really ask you to marry him?"

Why, oh why, had she felt the need to share that awkward moment? "It was just a joke."

Wasn't it?

Allegra frowned. "He's awfully intense. I don't get the impression he jokes around much, but I don't know him very well. Before the accident, we only saw him at recitals."

Before the accident?

Chloe swallowed. She wanted to press for more information, but at the same time, she was afraid to know more.

"It's so sad what happened, isn't it?" Allegra's voice went quiet, and the fear in the pit of Chloe's stomach crystallized into an overwhelming sense of dread. "To think that just a week ago, Lolly's mom was dropping her off at class. And now that sweet little girl is an orphan."

The Windex bottle nearly slipped through Chloe's fingers. "An orphan," she repeated woodenly.

"All because of a car accident. It's *tragic*. I suppose Anders will be appointed as her guardian since Grant was his brother, but you probably know all about that since the two of you are clearly acquainted." Allegra took the bottle of cleaner from Chloe's hands and put it back in the tiny storage cabinet in the corner of the classroom, oblivious to the fact that she'd suddenly become paralyzed.

A car accident.

It explained so much. It might even explain the out-of-the-blue proposal, although there had to be more to the story there. It *certainly* explained why Anders had been at the animal shelter to adopt a fluffy little puppy.

He'd been trying to comfort his niece. The dog had probably been Lolly's Christmas gift. He'd said so himself, hadn't he? And Chloe had been so wrapped up in her own problems that she'd chastised him for giving a puppy away as a present. She'd actually lectured him about responsible pet ownership, and he hadn't said a word. He'd just handed over the little dog and walked away.

"Anders is raising Lolly now, isn't he?" Allegra asked.

"Yes," Chloe said, as if she had intimate knowledge of the situation.

She didn't need anyone to tell her the truth. Deep down, she knew. Anders had lost his brother, and now he was suddenly a single dad to a grieving five-year-old little girl—a little girl who might have gotten a tiny Yorkie puppy for Christmas, if not for Chloe.

Who's the puppy thief now?

Chapter Five

"You wanted to see me?"

Anders closed his laptop and aimed his full attention at Penelope Reed hovering in the doorway of his office the following morning. "Yes. Please come in. Have a seat."

A fly on the wall would never suspect the two of them had ever shared a bed, but that was by design. Anders and Penelope weren't a couple, just two people who'd come to an understanding that suited them both. Which made him all the more convinced he was making the right choice.

Penelope would be the perfect wife, and the more he thought about it, the more convinced he'd become that no one at the office would even have to know. They could keep things private, and the marriage could simply be an extension of the unspoken agreement they already had. An addendum with mutually agreed upon terms and, most important, an expiration date.

She took a seat in one of the wingback chairs facing his desk, just as she'd done a thousand times before to discuss a stock offering or a merger.

"You look well, Anders. I'm happy you're back in the office." She shifted her gaze to her hands, folded neatly in her lap. "Apologies for not making it to the funeral. We had the Remington IPO, and I couldn't get away."

"I understand." Anders nodded.

In all honesty, her absence hadn't registered. He'd barely been aware of his surroundings on the day he'd buried Grant and Olivia. But it was fine. Penelope had never been the touchy-feely type, and there was no reason for that to change now.

But as he pulled open the top drawer of his desk, he heard the singsong lilt in Chloe Wilde's voice as she'd spoken to Lolly at the dance school the day before. He remembered the way Lolly had gazed up at her, eyes shining bright.

Are you a Christmas princess?

Penelope cleared her throat. "So what can I do for you?"

Anders's jaw tensed, and he pushed the sentimental memory away. *Focus.*

He needed someone reliable on his side. Someone he trusted. And that someone was most definitely *not* his niece's effusive dance teacher.

Besides, she'd already turned him down. And he was perfectly *fine* with her refusal. Relieved, actually.

"I have a proposal I wanted to discuss with you." Best to get right down to it. He'd wasted enough time in the past few days. "A business proposal…of sorts."

"I'm all ears." Penelope tilted her head.

She was a beautiful woman. No doubt about it. If Anders remembered correctly, she'd been a model for a few years before she'd gone to business school—in Paris, maybe. Or Tokyo. He wasn't quite sure.

But it was a flawless, cool kind of beauty, like one of Alfred Hitchcock's iconic blondes. Strange how he'd never noticed that before.

"I've prepared a contract for your review." He reached for the voluminous document that had been sitting in his drawer all morning like a bomb waiting to detonate, and his gaze snagged on the bold lettering printed across the margin of the top page.

Premarital Agreement.

His mouth went dry.

Why was this so difficult? He'd known Penelope for years. He'd proposed to Chloe within minutes of setting eyes on her, so asking Penelope to marry him should have been no trouble at all.

But he'd been shell-shocked from the meeting with the estate attorney when he'd hastily asked Chloe to be his wife. And it hadn't been a *genuine* proposal. He'd given more thought to what he'd had for lunch that day.

"So…" Penelope shifted in her chair and glanced at the vintage Tiffany desk clock on his credenza.

Anders smoothed down his tie and slid the contract toward her across the glossy surface of his desk. "It's all spelled out right here. The terms are negotiable, of course, other than the provisions spelled out in Section One."

She reached for the contract, but her hand froze midair as her gaze moved over the top of the page.

Clearly, he should have done a better job of preparing her for what was coming, but he was tired of putting it off, tired of sleepless nights, tired of wondering if he'd run out of time and Lolly would be taken away before the Christmas windows on Fifth Avenue came down.

So very, very tired.

"Anders, I don't understand." Penelope shook her head. "What is this? You want to marry me?"

No, actually. I don't.

He took a deep breath. "I need to get married. For Lolly."

"Oh." She gave him a thin-lipped smile. "So you're looking for a mommy figure for your orphaned niece."

"No. That's not it at all." He struggled to keep his tone even and businesslike.

He didn't care for her callous description of Lolly, but technically, it was true. And he'd botched enough marriage proposals in the past forty-eight hours to realize this one was off to a bad start. He needed a *yes*, whether he wanted one or not.

"In order to secure Lolly's guardianship, I have to be married by the end of the year," he said.

"The end of *this* year?" Penelope's brows crept up higher on her forehead.

"Yes." He nodded and took her stunned silence as the opportunity he needed to explain things. He laid out every detail of his proposed arrangement, from duration to compensation.

"Look," he concluded. "I know it's a lot to ask, but I don't have much time and I trust you, Penelope. We've successfully navigated a personal relationship for a while now, and I think we could make this transition rather seamlessly, in a way that could be beneficial to us both."

He leaned back in his chair and tried not to think about what Grant would have had to say about such a proposal. A lot, probably. But he was doing what needed to be done, the only way he knew how. And to his great relief, Penelope nodded instead of renegotiating the terms. Now all they had to do was sign the paperwork and make an appointment at city hall.

But when he offered her the Mont Blanc pen from his suit pocket, she refused to take it.

"No," she said quietly and pushed the contract away before removing her fingertips from the edge of the crisp white pages, as if they'd burned her skin.

Anders frowned. "What do you mean, *no*?"

"I mean *no*." She stood. "I'm sorry, Anders. But I just can't do it."

"May I ask why not?" he asked calmly.

Too calmly.

He should be panicked right now. Christmas was in

three short weeks, and he wasn't any closer to being married than he was two days ago.

But inexplicably, the knot of emotion in his chest felt more like relief than alarm.

It shouldn't be like this.

Even Anders knew this wasn't the way to choose a bride. Marriage was supposed to be a sacred vow, a lifetime commitment.

"I'm not cut out to be anyone's mommy, not even temporarily." Penelope shrugged. "And call me crazy, but if and when I get married someday, I want it to be for love."

Anders nodded. Maybe Penelope was more of a romantic than he'd realized.

Maybe you are, too.

He rubbed his eyes. Stress and exhaustion were messing with his head, not to mention the grief he was still doing his best to ignore. He'd grieve properly later, though. Once Lolly's guardianship was secure, he could grieve all he wanted.

Doesn't that sound like a joyous Christmas?

Christmas was the absolute last thing he had time for. If it were possible, Anders would snap his fingers and skip the rest of December altogether. No twinkling lights. No presents. No Christmas, period.

He sighed, opened his eyes and immediately wondered if the universe was playing some kind of joke on him. Or maybe he'd lost what little was left of his sanity, because he was suddenly seeing things.

Specifically, Chloe Wilde.

Standing in his office.

Dressed in her reindeer costume.

"Knock, knock," Chloe said, deflating a little beneath the weight of Anders's stare. "I hope I'm not interrupting anything."

She was *definitely* interrupting something. She had no idea what, but if the tense knot in Anders's jaw was any indication, it was big.

"You know what—never mind." She held Prancer's dog carrier more tightly against her chest. A barrier. "I'll come back later."

Or never.

This had been a monumentally bad idea. She should have just gone straight to Times Square for her afternoon flyer shift and forgotten about Anders Kent and his sad story altogether. Clearly, he didn't want her help.

"Wait." The woman standing beside Anders's desk held up an elegant hand. "Don't go. Mr. Kent and I are finished."

Chloe had no idea who the woman was, but she was gorgeous. Poised and classic, like a woman in a perfume commercial. Her polished chignon and sleek pencil skirt made Chloe even more aware that she was clad in brown faux Rudolph fur, if such a thing was even possible.

Plus, when the woman cast a final glance at Anders on the way out of his office, there was a quiet intimacy in her gaze that made Chloe's stomach churn.

She wasn't jealous. She couldn't be.

This impromptu visit had nothing to do with attraction. She was finished with dating after the Steven fiasco, and Anders Kent wasn't even her type. He was arrogant. He was also too cranky, too rich and far too handsome.

Although he had every right to be cranky, she thought with a pang.

Anyway, she was here for one reason and one reason only—to make things right.

"Miss Wilde," he said, once they were alone, and there was a weariness in his tone that made her heart ache.

She wished she could turn back the clock and go back to the afternoon at the animal shelter two days ago. If she'd known then what she knew now, she would have let him take the puppy. Only a monster would snatch a dog away from a child who'd just lost her parents.

Who's the puppy thief now?

But that was impossible, obviously. She wasn't George Bailey. She couldn't go back in time and do things differently. All she could do was let Lolly have Prancer.

"Here." She moved closer to Anders and set the pet carrier on his desk.

He looked at Prancer, and Chloe could hear the tiny dog's tail beating happily against the inside of the bag. "Perhaps you're mistaken, Miss Wilde. This is an investment banking firm, not a doggy day care."

Honestly, did he have to make this so difficult?

"Very funny. Look, I'm sorry to barge in here like

this, but I was afraid if I didn't do it now, I'd chicken out and change my mind."

He studied her, and her cheeks burned with heat. She started sweating beneath the fur of her reindeer costume.

"Change your mind about what, exactly?" he said.

He truly didn't get it, did he?

"Prancer." She waved a hand at the dog, now attempting to break free from the pet carrier and crawl toward Anders across the paper-strewn desk. "The puppy. I want Lolly to have her."

His gaze softened, and for a brief, silvery moment, she caught a glimpse of sadness in the cool blue depths of his eyes, an emotion so profound, so hopeless, that her breath caught in her throat.

Then, as quickly as it had appeared, that heartbreaking flash of vulnerability was gone, and his chiseled face was once again a perfect, impenetrable mask.

"You named the puppy Prancer," he said flatly. "Why does that not surprise me a bit?"

She sat down in one of the stuffy chairs opposite him. Not that he'd offered. "I did, but Lolly can rename her if she likes."

Her throat grew thick, and she pasted on a smile. Giving up the puppy wasn't going to be easy. She'd grown attached to the little ball of fur, especially since she'd helped bottle-feed Prancer when she was still at the shelter, too young to be adopted out.

But she'd be damned if Anders Kent would know how much she'd miss the precious little dog.

He shook his head, and his voice dropped an octave until it was low and deep enough to scrape her insides. “That won’t be necessary.”

“If she wants to keep the name, that’s fine, too…”

“No.” He shook his head again, and shockingly, his mouth curved into a smile. It was a Christmas miracle! “I mean I want you to keep the dog. I’ve found another puppy for Lolly. In fact, I’m stopping by the shelter this evening to pick her up.”

“Oh, I see. Well, that’s…” She swallowed. “…wonderful.”

It *was* wonderful. It was the best possible news, given the circumstances. But for some strange reason, it struck Chloe as bittersweet.

“I appreciate the offer, though,” Anders said. And then he looked at her again—*really* looked—until she forgot all about her silly reindeer costume and her derby hat with its velvet antlers and felt as if she was bared before him. An unwrapped gift.

She took a shaky inhalation and dropped her gaze.

That was when she saw it.

Premarital Agreement.

She stared at the words on the document sitting on Anders’s desk until they swam together, forming a dark, inky pool. “What’s this?”

None of your business, that’s what.

Anders cleared his throat. “It’s nothing.”

Chloe stared at him until he looked away, and then she thought about the lovely woman who’d been standing beside his desk when she’d arrived. She thought about how natural the two of them had looked together, how perfectly matched they'd seemed. Like two blue-blooded peas in a pod.

"You're getting married?" she sputtered. The words were out of her mouth before she could stop them, and to her horror, they were laced with hurt.

She had no right to be upset. Still, what did the man do? Propose to every woman he met?

"No." Anders shook his head, then grimaced. "I mean, yes."

After a pause, he added, "I think."

Chloe lifted a brow. "How can you not know?"

"It's complicated." He reached for the sheaf of papers on the desk in front of her, but not before Chloe saw the names printed in the first paragraph.

This agreement is made by and between Anders Kent and Penelope Reed...

Below that, she saw a substantial dollar amount, which didn't quite make sense. He wanted to *pay* someone to marry him?

Chloe knew better than to ask any more questions. None of this was her business. But she couldn't seem to stop herself.

"Penelope Reed." She turned the name over in her mind. It sounded very sophisticated, very posh—the perfect sort of name for a bride someone like Anders would choose, as opposed to a person he'd only temporarily propose to. "Let me guess—that's the woman who was just in here, wasn't it."

He shoved the contract in one of the desk drawers and slammed it closed. "I'm not marrying Penelope Reed."

"But it was her, wasn't it?" Why did she care? More important, why was she still sitting here? She had less than an hour to get to Times Square, and the subway would be packed this time of day.

Anders sighed. "Yes, it was."

"And she turned you down?"

He glared at her.

"I'll take that as a yes."

"Look, Miss Wilde. I appreciate your offer regarding the dog. It was very thoughtful, but I have a lot on my plate right now..."

"Like finding a wife?" She couldn't resist. Something strange was going on, and she had to know what it was. And when she really thought about it, it sort of *was* her business, since for a split second, she'd been on his list of potential brides. "Why do you want to get married so badly, anyway? And why on earth would you offer someone money to be your wife?"

He narrowed his gaze at her. "Do you always ask so many questions?"

"Do you always propose to every woman who crosses your path?" she countered.

He crossed his arms, and she caught a glimpse of the crisp French cuffs of his shirt, his understated platinum cuff links and just a sliver of his manly wrists. Her heart beat hard, and she looked away.

Who in their right mind got swoony over a man's wrist?

"If I tell you, will you and Prancer dash on out of here so I can get some work done?" He shot an amused glance at her antlers.

She shrugged one shoulder. “Maybe.”

Definitely. If she didn’t leave in exactly ten minutes, she’d be late for work.

Again, what was she still doing, sitting there in his office?

“I can’t be appointed as Lolly’s permanent guardian unless I’m married. I’ve got until Christmas to find a wife.” He lifted a brow. “Happy now? Any more questions?”

So this was about Lolly.

Chloe’s indignation melted away, replaced by a feeling much more complex, much more bittersweet. She couldn’t quite put her finger on what it was, but it made her heart beat hard in her chest. And it made her think that maybe, just maybe, she could help Anders and his sweet little niece.

Plus, that dollar amount on the contract would go a long way toward improving the dance school.

“Just one.” *This is crazy.* She swallowed. *Don’t do it. Just get up and leave. Walk away while you still can.* But she knew she wouldn’t—couldn’t if she’d tried. “Why not me?”

Chapter Six

He didn't have a choice.

At least that was what Anders told himself when he agreed to marry Chloe Wilde. It was also what he told himself when she'd left Prancer in his care so she could go to work in her reindeer costume, which made for an interesting afternoon at the office. The havoc wrought by the Yorkie as Anders made conference calls and met with clients was astounding, especially given the dog's tiny size.

He'd had to call the animal shelter and cancel yet another pending puppy adoption, which meant he'd probably be blackballed from getting another pet for the rest of his life. But adding a wife and a dog to his household right after it had doubled in size seemed like more than enough to deal with at the moment.

On some level, he was aware that he could have said no. No to babysitting Chloe's dog. No to at least some of the chaos, but for reasons he didn't care to examine too closely, he hadn't. It was easier to keep believing that all the recent upheaval in his life was out of his control. Lolly needed him, therefore he needed Chloe. Again, he didn't have a choice.

But applying for a marriage license the following morning *felt* like one, especially when Chloe turned up to meet him on the front steps of the city clerk's office on Worth Street wearing a winter-white swing coat over a pretty pleated dress, and a flower tucked into her upswept hair. It occurred to him as he climbed the building's sweeping marble steps and made his way toward her that he'd never seen her in anything but her reindeer costume or dance clothes. And now here she was, looking as lovely as ever.

Like a bride.

His bride.

"Hi." She gave him an uncharacteristically bashful smile, and he was suddenly acutely aware of the sound of his own heartbeat, pounding relentlessly in his ears.

"Hi. You look..." He paused when he realized his hands were shaking, and tucked them into the pockets of his overcoat. "...beautiful."

"Thank you." Her cheeks flared pink. "I know we're not actually getting married today, only getting the license, but I figured I should probably look the part. Just a little, so it seems real. You know?"

Mission accomplished. Once they had the license

and waited the mandatory twenty-four hours, they'd be husband and wife. It didn't get much more real than that.

"Look, I know we didn't discuss this, but I think it would be best if we kept things between us strictly platonic from here on out," she said, without meeting his gaze. "Don't you agree?"

"Absolutely." Inside his coat pockets, his hands balled into fists.

"So, no sex." At last she looked him in the eyes.

He held her gaze until the flush in her cheeks turned berry red. "I know what *platonic* means."

"Right." She swallowed, and he traced the movement up and down the slender column of her throat. "Just so we're clear."

"Crystal." It was a perfectly reasonable request, and if she hadn't brought it up, he definitely would have. The surest way to screw everything up would be to sleep together. But having it spelled out for him so succinctly was more unpleasant than he wanted to admit.

"I mean, not that we would have. You probably don't even want to."

"I don't," he lied.

"Perfect." She nodded. Snow flurries had begun to gather in her hair, and paired with the white blooms in her loosely gathered ballerina bun, it made her look like something out of a fairy tale. A Snow Queen. "Neither do I."

He wondered if she was lying, too, but then reminded himself it didn't matter because they wouldn't be going there under any circumstances. "It's settled, then. No sex."

"Good." Her gaze dropped to his mouth.

Yep, she's lying, too. He couldn't help but smile, despite the absurdity of the situation. "Good."

He nodded toward the building's revolving gilt door, where a bride and groom spun their way outside and stopped for a passionate kiss in the gently falling snow. "Shall we go in?"

Her gaze snagged on the couple. Then her lush lips parted, ever so softly. And damned if Anders didn't go hard.

What was happening?

She was gorgeous, but he'd known that all along. He'd been attracted to her since that first day at the animal shelter. If his life hadn't been such a spectacular mess at the moment, he would have no doubt acted on it by now.

But his life *was* a mess, and Chloe was the only person willing to help him straighten it out. Now wasn't the time for his libido to make an appearance after days of moving through life in a state of constant numbness.

"Yes, let's go." She brushed past him, and he inhaled a lungful of cold, cleansing air.

She'd mentioned sex, so now he was thinking about it. Plain and simple. His visceral reaction to her meant nothing whatsoever.

Sure it doesn't.

"Anders? Are you coming?" She glanced over her

shoulder, and her pleated skirt swirled around her willowy legs.

His arousal showed zero signs of ebbing. If anything, he grew harder. But he managed to put one foot in front of the other and follow her inside.

The foyer split into two different directions—weddings to the left, licenses to the right. Anders placed his hand on the small of Chloe's back and guided her to the proper line.

It was an innocent gesture, just the barest of touches, but it filled him with inexplicable heat. Every nerve ending in his body seemed to gather at the small point of contact between the tips of his fingers and the delicate arch of her spine.

He snatched his hand away and buried it back in his coat pocket as they took their place behind dozens of happily engaged couples.

This is a terrible idea. The worst.

He should have stuck with his original plan and found someone to marry who was safe. Someone who he wasn't attracted to in the slightest, and more important, someone who wasn't already part of Lolly's life. How would it be possible for them to make a clean break when all this was over?

One thing at a time, he reminded himself. All the logistics were spelled out in the premarital agreement. The contract was absolutely crucial. It would protect them both...if only he'd remembered it.

He closed his eyes and sighed. How could he have forgotten something so important? "Damn it."

"Anders." Chloe's hand landed lightly on his forearm. "Everything okay?"

No. Everything was *not* okay. They were standing in line for a marriage license, and he didn't even know her middle name. "I forgot the contract."

She blinked. "What contract?"

"The premarital agreement," he muttered under his breath. How many other couples in this queue were having a similar discussion? Zero, probably.

"Oh, I thought that was just something between you and…" Her voice drifted off.

"Penelope," he said.

"Right." Chloe stiffened. "Her."

He lifted a brow. Was she *jealous*? Surely not.

"What?" She lifted her chin, eyes glittering.

"Nothing. You just seem…" He bit back a smile. Anders knew a jealous woman when he saw one, but he didn't want to embarrass her. Nor did he want to get into another discussion even remotely related to sexual attraction. "Never mind."

Her gaze narrowed. "Okay, but what were you saying? About the agreement?"

The contract. He'd forgotten about it *again*. "I meant to redraft it and bring it along today so we could sign it. I thought it would be best to have a notary here at the city clerk's office serve as our witness instead of one from my office."

"Because you don't want anyone from your office to know we're getting married?"

"I don't see why it's necessary. Isn't the plan to get married on paper with as little disturbance to our daily lives as possible?" Why did saying this out loud make him feel like the world's biggest cad? "I think that's what's best for Lolly."

"You're probably right." Chloe nodded.

Their gazes met and held, until he finally took a deep breath and looked away. "All of this is spelled out in the contract."

"You mean the one you forgot to write?" she said wryly.

"Yes."

The line moved forward again, until only one couple stood between them and the little slip of paper that would give them legal permission to marry.

Chloe turned to face him, and for a split second, he wondered what waiting in this queue would have felt like if they'd been a real couple. Would they have held hands during the long wait? Would they have whispered promises to one another and made plans for their future? Would he have cupped her face and kissed her when they finally reached the point where they stood now, on the brink of swearing in front of a government official that they'd chosen one another, that they would soon exchange vows?

He would. He could imagine it, clear as day in his mind's eye—her heart-shaped face, tipped upward toward his, the softening in her gaze as he lowered his mouth to hers, her slight intake of breath before their lips met. He could picture it so vividly that it almost seemed like a memory instead of some alternate version of reality. A fantasy that would never come true.

"It's fine. Don't worry about the agreement. I'm

doing you a favor, and in return, you'll do one for me. The dance school can use that money." She smiled. "I trust you."

He gazed down at her and wondered if she had any inkling what those words meant to him. His own brother hadn't trusted him enough to grant him unconditional guardianship over Lolly, but Chloe was willing to walk down the aisle toward him without any sort of paperwork to protect her.

Anders was a stranger, and she was prepared to marry him. She could call it a favor if she liked, but they both knew it was more than that. So much more.

I trust you.

He reached for her hand and wove his fingers through hers. Somewhere deep inside him a dam was breaking, and he couldn't tell whether it was a good thing or a bad one, but didn't want to face it alone.

"Anders Astor Kent and Chloe Grace Wilde?" The clerk behind the counter looked up.

Chloe squeezed his hand as they stepped forward, and Anders realized he'd just learned something new, something serendipitous.

Grace.

His bride's middle name was Grace.

"How do you feel about Lolly Kent for the part of Clara?" Chloe slid the Tchaikovsky album back into its sleeve after *Baby Nutcracker* rehearsal the next day and did her best to sound nonchalant.

All the time she'd spent onstage must have made an actress out of her, because Allegra seemed oblivious.

"Sure." Allegra peeled her ballet shoes off and slid her feet into a pair of Uggs. "You're the director, remember. Emily put you in charge, and I'm just helping out. The casting is up to you."

Clara was the lead role, and while she wasn't technically a princess, whoever danced the part would be the star of the show. She'd also get to wear a tiara for most of the recital, which should satisfy Lolly's princess obsession.

"She's one of the oldest girls in the group, so I'm sure she could handle the simple choreography," Chloe said.

Allegra's gaze narrowed, ever so slightly.

"Plus, I just feel so bad for her, you know. She's only a little girl, and she's been through so much." Not to mention the fact that if she and Anders went through with the wedding, Lolly would sort of be her stepdaughter.

Her stomach did a little flip. *When* they went through with it, not *if.* They had the marriage license. Now it was simply a matter of waiting the mandatory twenty-four hours before they could go back to city hall and exchange vows.

It's really happening.

No one would know, obviously. She and Anders had agreed on that, for Lolly's sake. They'd decided not to tell anyone, except Anders's lawyer. It would be a marriage on paper only—a business transaction—for the sole purpose of satisfying the legal requirements for Lolly's guardianship. They weren't even going to share an apartment.

Which meant her awkward announcement that they wouldn't be sleeping together hadn't been necessary. Great. Now Anders probably thought she *wanted* to sleep with him. And she most definitely did *not*.

At least that was what she kept telling herself.

"Why are you still trying to convince me?" Allegra leaned her back against the ballet barre and crossed her arms. "I already told you it was fine."

"No reason." Chloe swallowed. Maybe she wasn't as talented acting-wise as she'd imagined.

"Are you sure? You're acting a little strange. Also, when Lolly's uncle came to pick her up just now, you two wouldn't even look at each other."

What were they supposed to do? Walk around in matching Bride and Groom T-shirts, joined at the hip? "There are a dozen kids in the *Baby Nutcracker* class. I'm sure I failed to make eye contact with a lot of the parents."

Allegra smirked. "Nope, just Anders Kent. It was almost like you were both going out of your way to avoid each other."

Probably because they were. Chloe was definitely doing her best to avoid Anders. She wasn't sure she was physically capable of standing an arm's length away from him in the dance studio, meeting his gaze and pretending he was only a casual acquaintance when he was about to be her husband.

Your fake *husband.*

Why did she keep having to remind herself that this crazy engagement wasn't even a tiny bit real?

"Stop looking at me like that." She scowled at Allegra. "I barely know Anders Kent."

"He was the lone man in a sea of frazzled moms just now. A distractingly hot man, at that. I find it hard to believe you didn't notice."

"Well, I didn't." Chloe looked up from her clip-board and flashed Allegra a knowing grin. "But I'll be sure to tell my brother you think Anders is hot."

As if Zander would care. He'd worshipped the ground Allegra walked on since they were kids. Now that they were married, he was even more besotted.

Allegra laughed. "I'm married to your brother, but I'm not blind. I'm head over heels for Zander. You know that."

Chloe rolled her eyes. "Yes, I do. It's actually a little nauseating how happy you two are. Thanks for the reminder."

"Which is why I think the gorgeous Mr. Kent might be perfect for *you*." Allegra's tone softened. "Unless you're not ready to date because you're upset about Steven. What happened between you, anyway?"

Chloe flinched, and her grip tightened on the clip-board. She hadn't thought about Steven in a while. Days, maybe. Agreeing to marry a stranger was a sur-prisingly effective strategy for navigating a breakup. But the shock of hearing her ex's name out of the blue was like pressing a tender bruise.

She swallowed. "It just wasn't going anywhere."

But they had *been* going somewhere. Chloe had even thought Steven might propose over the holidays. He'd dropped a few hints about a surprise during her upcoming Christmas Eve performance at Radio City. Like a lovesick fool, she'd imagined him down on bended knee in the darkened theater, slipping a ring onto her finger during the curtain call.

She'd been wrong, of course. So. Very. Wrong. He'd never planned on proposing. He'd simply wanted to bring some important business associates to the show. He'd wanted to use her to dazzle his clients, not marry her. Once she'd been dropped from the performance roster, he'd clued her in to the "surprise."

And then he'd dumped her like she was a kid on Santa's naughty list.

"I'm here if you ever need to talk." Allegra wrapped a slender arm around Chloe's shoulders. "You know that, right?"

A lump lodged in Chloe's throat. Steven was right. She definitely belonged on the naughty list. She still hadn't fessed up to her family, and now she was piling lies on top of lies by keeping them in the dark about her unconventional wedding.

But that was okay, right? Because soon she'd be able to fix the floors and paint the walls and finish what Allegra had started with the dance marathon, and really turn things around at the Wilde School of Dance.

Then it would no longer matter that she'd been MIA for the better part of four years and made a mess of her career on live television. She could make up for all her mistakes. All the little white lies.

She just had to hold on until Lolly's custody hearing.

"Thank you. I love knowing I can talk to you. I

really do, just like I'm grateful to Mom for the chance to help out around here."

"We're lucky to have you. You're a superstar!" Allegra nodded toward the lobby, where Chloe's smiling face beamed from the huge Rockettes poster. "Obviously, I hope your calf heals soon, but until it does, I love having you here. Plus, it gives Emily a little break."

Chloe couldn't bring herself to look at the poster anymore. She kept her gaze glued to her clipboard so she wouldn't be forced to face the constant reminder of how far her star had fallen. "Where is Mom, anyway?"

"She's supposed to be taking the day off, but if the vibrating phone in my pocket is any indication, she can't stand being away." Allegra reached into the pocket of her swishy ballet skirt and pulled out her cell phone. "Oh my God, she called four times during the past hour, even though she knew we had class."

"That's weird. I hope nothing's wrong." Dread snaked its way up Chloe's spine. She reached for her iPhone, where she'd placed it beside the record player.

The screen lit up with notifications. Six missed calls and three texts, all from her mother. "She's been trying to reach me, too."

Something definitely wasn't right.

"I've got a voice mail." Allegra pressed her phone to her ear, and after a second or two, her eyes widened and focused intently on Chloe.

She wasn't sure what the look meant, and she was genuinely afraid to ask. Instead, she scrolled through

Emily's text messages. But instead of clearing things up, they left her more confused than ever.

Have you seen the paper today?

The paper?

The *New York Times*...they've made some kind of mistake.

Chloe was vaguely aware of Allegra saying something beside her, but she couldn't focus on the exact words. Her mother was obviously freaking out about something she'd seen in the *Times*, which could mean only one thing—they'd identified her as the dancer who'd ruined the Rockettes' most famous number during the Macy's parade.

Why now, though? Thanksgiving had been over a week ago.

She took a deep breath. Whatever article had gotten Emily all stirred up must be about something else. But what could be so urgent that she'd made multiple calls to both her and Allegra while she knew they were teaching the *Baby Nutcracker* class?

Chloe flipped to the next text message, hoping for clarity. But when she saw the shouty caps filling her screen, she froze and remembered the old adage—be careful what you wish for.

I KNOW YOU WOULDN'T BE PLANNING ON GETTING MARRIED WITHOUT TELLING YOUR FAMILY.

She glanced up, heart pounding so hard and fast she almost couldn't breathe.

"I knew there was something going on between you and Anders Kent," Allegra said. And then she laughed. She actually *laughed*, as if Chloe wasn't about to drop dead from panic right in front of her. "But *engaged*? Already? The other day, when you said he'd proposed, I thought you were joking. Emily is about to come unglued. I could barely understand her voice mail message, but I managed to catch the fact that you're getting married. You've got some explaining to do."

Oh God.

"I..." Her mouth opened and then closed. What could she possibly say?

He's paying me to marry him.

Technically, that was the truth. But wow, put so bluntly, it sounded terrible. Really, really terrible.

"You what?" Allegra lifted a brow.

Before Chloe could form a response, her phone pinged with another incoming text.

From Emily...again.

I'm on my way. I'll be there in five minutes or less.

Chapter Seven

Emily must have been moving at the speed of light because she burst through the door of the dance school less than sixty seconds after Chloe received her text message.

Granted, it had been a long sixty seconds—the longest, most excruciating minute of her life as Allegra stared her down, waiting to hear all about how Chloe had managed to become engaged to a man she hadn't so much as spoken to when he'd come to pick up his daughter just moments ago. A man who she claimed was a total stranger.

"It's sort of a crazy story," Chloe said, pressing the heel of her hand against her breastbone.

Her heart was beating so hard she thought she might be having a coronary. She almost wished she were. At least if her heart stopped beating, Emily would forget about whatever she'd read in the paper that led her to believe Chloe and Anders were getting married.

Probably.

Or probably not.

Emily pushed through the door, clutching a copy of the *New York Times* to her chest and out of breath. Her coat wasn't even buttoned. By all appearances, she'd either speed-walked or run all the way to the school from the brownstone.

"Oh boy," Allegra muttered under her breath.

Yeah. Chloe pressed harder on her breastbone, lest her heart beat right out of her chest. *Oh boy.*

"Chloe, what's going on? This columnist, Celestia Lane, made some sort of mistake, right? Or was it intentional erroneous reporting? Isn't she the reporter who made life so miserable for Zander last year?" Emily tossed the paper onto the reception desk and there, in black and white across the top of the popular *Vows* column, was the headline Manhattan Billionaire Anders Kent Granted Marriage License.

Manhattan billionaire?

Chloe didn't know billionaires were an actual thing. She thought they existed only in *Batman* movies and romance novels. No wonder he seemed so hung up on the premarital agreement. He probably thought she was trying to con him or something when she'd told him not to worry about it.

As if that was her most pressing worry at the moment. Chloe's name was in the very first sentence of the article, for the entire world to see. People all over the world read the *Vows* column, not just New York. It was famous for its Sunday coverage of all the society weddings and celebrity engagements. Sometimes during the week it contained juicy matrimonial gossip.

Like now.

"That's definitely the same reporter." Allegra rolled her eyes. "She ran that whole series of columns about the Bennington and tried to make everyone believe it was cursed. This is obviously fake news. Why didn't you just say so, Chloe?"

She paused for a beat and then added, "It's kind of weird that the reporter used your name, though, out of all the women in New York."

Chloe took a deep breath. "It's not fake news. Not this time."

Celestia Lane definitely had a penchant for exaggerating. Zander's hotel had nearly gone bankrupt, all because she'd penned a series of articles about the Bennington's unusually high number of runaway brides. Allegra herself had been one of the brides who'd famously bolted from the hotel ballroom in a puffy white gown.

But that was a long time ago. The columnist may have manufactured the runaway bride curse, but this time her information was spot-on.

"So you're really marrying Anders Kent?" Allegra's jaw dropped.

Emily didn't say a word, and somehow her rigid posture and sudden silence was worse than if she'd yelled or screamed. But Chloe's mom had never been that kind of parent. It took a lot to make her upset, and when she finally reached her breaking point, she was much more likely to issue a calm, low reprimand than to raise her voice.

The fact that she couldn't seem to form words at all was definitely a bad sign. The worst.

"Mom, I can explain..." Could she, though? Could she really?

The phone in Chloe's hand pinged with a text, and she nearly dropped it. She'd forgotten she was even holding her cell until her cheery "Jingle Bells" text tone pierced the tense silence.

At last, Emily found her voice. "Who is it? Your secret fiancé?"

Chloe glanced down.

We need to talk. Meet me at Soho House at earliest possible opportunity? I'll send a driver to collect you.

Anders, indeed.

But he wasn't such a secret anymore.

So much for keeping things simple.

The news piece in the *Times* changed everything. As Anders's attorney so bluntly put it, everything about his relationship with Chloe needed to look real. Not just the wedding, but the marriage.

Everything.

Assuming, of course, that Chloe would still go through with their arrangement. Anders had a feeling she wouldn't, especially when she showed up at the Soho House looking every bit as shell-shocked as he felt.

Meeting her here suddenly seemed like a bad idea. If this was the end of their brief fake relationship, he'd much rather have ended things privately at his office instead of a trendy eatery. Soho House was a members-only establishment, but it was still filled with prying eyes. Three people had congratulated Anders on his engagement since he'd arrived ten minutes before.

"Hello." He rose from the table as she approached.

"Hi." She came around to his side of the table and wrapped her arms around him, enveloping him in a scent reminiscent of warm vanilla with just a touch of evergreen. Christmas on a snowy morning.

He had a sudden flash of memories from his childhood—the kind of Christmas mornings he hadn't experienced in years, with fresh baked cookies, a fire in the hearth and frost on the windows. They were the sort of memories he should be making for Lolly, especially now. What if he never had the chance again? What if this was the last Christmas she'd ever spend in New York?

Don't go there.

Chloe pressed her lips, impossibly soft, against his cheek, and as ludicrous as it seemed, that simple, innocent brush of her skin against his almost made him feel like everything might be okay. Like he could somehow keep Lolly's world—and his—from falling apart.

She pulled back and looked at him with wide, nervous eyes. Her voice dropped to a low murmur. "I hope that was okay. I just feel like since we're out in public and now everyone knows..."

Her cheeks blazed pink, and for the first time since he'd set eyes on the *Vows* column, the dull ache in his temples eased. The knot in his chest loosened, and he could breathe again. He wasn't sure why. According to his lawyer, Lolly's custody case had just gotten infinitely more complicated. Even if Chloe was still willing to walk down the aisle, they would have to pass for a believable couple until nearly the end of the month.

Until Christmas.

"It's fine." He slipped her hand in his, gave it a squeeze and then pulled back her chair. "Please, have a seat. Relax."

Relax...easier said than done. Although when he took his place beside her, Anders could imagine how nice it might be to spend time with her under normal circumstances. They'd been together only a handful of times, but he was already becoming accustomed to the way she moved—with a willowy grace that made even the simplest gestures more lovely. It soothed him somehow.

He took a deep inhalation and met her gaze with his. "I'm sorry."

A little furrow formed between her brows. "You're apologizing?"

Apparently, he was. He hadn't planned on it, but suddenly it seemed like a good idea. Necessary, even. "Yes, for the article. I had no idea it was going to happen, but on some level, I feel like I should have seen it coming."

Her gaze shifted to the menu sitting untouched on the table in front of her. "It's not your fault."

"The tabloids have taken an interest in my personal life in the past." He shook his head. "Still, I never expected this. The *Times*, for crying out loud. *Vows*."

"Seriously, don't blame yourself. It's as much my fault as it is yours." Her eyes met his again and held.

He hadn't a clue what she was talking about, but he was struck once again by the sadness in her eyes, just as he'd been at the animal shelter. But he realized now it was more than melancholy. Secrets swirled in the depths of her soft brown irises, and he reminded himself that, loveliness aside, he knew nothing about this woman.

Other than she's your only hope.

"Why would it be your fault?" Had she gone to the press?

Surely not. He felt guilty even suspecting her of doing such a thing.

"The reporter who wrote the piece did a series of articles about my brother's hotel a year ago. He's the CEO of the Bennington."

"The runaway bride curse?" He nodded. "She mentioned it in the article."

"Right. That's why I think it's my fault. I just can't figure out how she knew we were engaged."

Anders sighed. "As my attorney was quick to point out this morning, marriage licenses are public record. Anyone can look them up at the city clerk's office."

"Oh." Chloe's bottom lip slid between her teeth and despite everything—despite the fact that he still expected her to bow out of their agreement as soon as she'd heard the lawyer's assessment of their situation, despite the fact that Anders's well-ordered life was slipping slowly into an abyss and despite the fact that he'd sworn to himself not to touch her—he went still. Spellbound. And as much as he knew he shouldn't be aroused at a time like this, it was so damn nice just to *feel* again.

He'd been growing accustomed to the numbness associated with grief. He'd welcomed it. So long as he had work to do and problems to sort out—so long as he remained distracted and blissfully detached from his loss—he was fine. He could hold it together, and he could push away the memories of the things he'd said to his brother and the way Grant had looked at him before he'd stalked out of the office one final time.

There was a price to pay for that kind of numbness, though. Other things got lost in the hazy, unfeeling blur of his new existence. Things like joy. Laughter.

Lust.

He shouldn't want Chloe Wilde. He couldn't—not if he had a chance in hell of keeping his tiny, two-person family intact. But every so often, she had a way of making him feel alive again. And when it happened, it was like breaking through the surface of a deep, dark pool and taking the first gasping breath of air. It burned, but at the same time, it kept him going…gave him hope.

"So what happens, exactly?" she asked, and he

forced his attention away from her mouth and back to her soulful eyes. "Do reporters sift through the marriage license records every day, trying to find newsworthy engagements?"

He gave her a grim smile. "That's exactly what they do, but don't blame yourself. I have a feeling Celestia Lane is far more interested in my recent family drama than your connection to the Bennington. From the looks of the article, she wants to paint me as some kind of romantic figure—a groom in mourning, saved by love."

The server approached their table, and Anders was grateful for the interruption. He hadn't brought Chloe here for a heart-to-heart. But as soon as he'd chosen a wine and they'd placed their orders, the waiter slipped away and they were alone again, with his words hanging between them.

A groom in mourning...

"Do you want to talk about it?" Chloe leaned closer, and the earnestness in her gaze made it impossible for him to cut her off.

The other women in his life knew better than to look at him like that—he wasn't an open book. Never had been, never would be. Which was precisely why his businesslike arrangement with Penelope worked out so nicely. Or it *had*, anyway.

"No, I don't want to talk about it. I—" His voice broke, and damn it if something inside him didn't break along with it.

He reached for his freshly poured wine and took a long swallow. When he placed his glass back down on the table, Chloe was still watching him with those tender eyes of hers, waiting for him to finish.

"Grant and I had an argument," he heard himself say. He couldn't stop himself; the truth just came spilling out. "The night of the car crash, before he left the office, we exchanged words. It got ugly."

"Anders, your relationship with your brother is made up of a lifetime of moments, not just his last day. Whatever happened, it's okay." She reached across the table and rested her hand on his. He held on tight to her fingertips, reluctant to release them, so he wouldn't have to sit there so excruciatingly alone after his confession.

Of all people, why her? He could have bared his soul to anyone, but instead he'd just told his darkest secret to his stranger fiancé. He wanted to believe it was so that she'd sympathize with him so much that she wouldn't walk away, that she'd stick by him and marry him even though the stakes had just risen dramatically.

But deep down he knew better. She was going to be his wife. For better or worse, she needed to know what she was getting into, even temporarily.

"I told him he was too focused on his family and he needed to spend more of his energy on work. Specifically, I said, 'You've got all the time in the world. Family can wait.'" Anders slid his hand away from hers and gripped the stem of his wineglass. The dark liquid sloshed perilously close to the rim in his trembling grasp. "Right before he walked out, he called me a monster."

He had to give Chloe credit; she didn't even flinch. Her expression remained as calm and pure as ever. Like a Christmas angel. Then she took a deep breath and said, "I got fired on Thanksgiving Day, and I've been lying to my family ever since."

Anders nearly choked on his Bordeaux. "What?"

"I messed up the legendary toy soldier routine." Her face went as red as a poinsettia. "You might have seen the video. It sort of went viral."

He nodded. "I think I did."

He knew what she was doing. She was trying to assuage his guilt by confessing to her own deep, dark secret. And her transgression was mild compared to his, so it shouldn't have worked. Somehow, it still did. Just a little bit.

"So yeah, I'm not actually a Rockette anymore. My mom and Allegra think I'm working at the studio now because I have a calf injury. I lied to both of their faces. You're the only one who knows the truth." She stared into her wineglass. "Except for Steven, but he doesn't matter anymore."

There was that name again. Steven. The ex.

Anders couldn't help but wonder if the mysterious Steven truly no longer mattered. He hoped not. Purely for the sake of their arrangement, of course.

Liar. That's not the only reason.

"Can I ask you a question?" he said.

"Sure."

"What about the reindeer costume? Is that part of a cover-up, or do you simply enjoy wearing it?"

There was a beat of silence. Then the sound of her

bell-like laughter broke through the somber mood that had settled over the table.

"The truth is more pathetic than you can imagine. I hand out flyers in Times Square for the Rockettes Christmas show." She smiled at him over her wineglass.

He winced. "Ouch."

"Trust me, it's as bad as you think it is. But it's a paycheck, and I keep thinking maybe I'll get back on the performance roster if they see how devoted I am."

The waiter returned with their food, and while he set their plates on the table, Anders tried to imagine standing in Times Square in costume for an afternoon. He wouldn't last a minute.

"So you'd go back to performing if you had the chance?" he asked, once they were alone again.

"Of course I would. Why wouldn't I?"

"I don't know." He shrugged. "You seem great with the kids at the dance studio. Lolly adores you."

Chloe grew quiet again, and the lightness of the moment faded away. The mention of Lolly had dragged them back to reality. For a moment it had felt like they were a regular couple out on a date, but they weren't.

"She adores you, too. You *do* know that, don't you?" Chloe's eyes shone bright in the warm glow of the restaurant. Behind her, snow beat against the window, and the sidewalk outside bustled with people carrying red and gold shopping bags. "Families are complicated. I never met your brother, but I know he loved you. If he didn't, he never would have left Lolly in your care. Not even conditionally."

But the condition was big, and it was time to tell her just how much of a commitment their fake marriage was going to entail.

He took a deep breath and then spelled it all out. "The article in the paper changes things. I met with my lawyer this morning and he said the press coverage of our engagement could look like a warning sign to the judge in the custody case. If we do this, it needs to look real. We'd have to have an actual wedding ceremony instead of getting married at city hall. And we'd have to do it immediately. Tomorrow, if possible. Afterward, you'd need to move into my apartment. From the outside, we'd have to look like newlyweds. At least until the custody hearing."

She had only one question. "Would I be able to tell my family the truth?"

Anders shook his head. "No, absolutely not. If the guardianship hearing doesn't go well, they might eventually be asked to testify in court."

"Okay." She nodded.

"Okay to the part about your family or okay to all of it?"

She took a deep breath. "All of it."

He angled his head. "You're absolutely sure?"

She nodded again. This was officially the easiest negotiation Anders had ever been a part of.

"Why are you doing this? You don't even know me." His gaze narrowed.

"Honestly, I could use the money. I'm unemployed at the moment, remember?" Her gaze shifted to her lap. "Besides, you seem like a decent person, and

Lolly is precious. I know what it's like to lose a father. I wasn't as young as Lolly is now, but I want to help her. I want to help you both."

"Thank you," he said, and it felt wholly inadequate, but it was all he had to offer her.

Except that wasn't quite true. There was one other thing…

He reached into the inside pocket of his suit jacket, pulled out a little blue box tied with a white satin ribbon and slid it toward her across the table.

She stared at it and smiled, but didn't make a move to touch it.

Anders had never seen a woman afraid of a box from Tiffany's before. "Open it. It's yours."

She picked it up. Hesitated. "Can I ask you something first?"

And here it was—the moment when she changed her mind. Anders couldn't blame her. If he'd been in her position, he would have walked away before the appetizers arrived.

At least he thought he would. He wasn't quite sure of anything where Chloe was concerned.

"Ask away," he said.

She looked at the ring box and then back up at him. "Is this part of the contract?"

It wasn't, and suddenly that fact seemed significant.

He lifted a brow. "You mean the contract that still doesn't exist?"

She nodded. "Yep, that's one."

"Of course," he lied. "Just part of the package."

Because how could he tell her the truth? How could he admit that he'd bought her an engagement ring just because he'd wanted to? He'd managed to convince himself that it was no big deal. She was going to be his wife, after all. But the fact that he was trying to pass it off as part of a clause in a contract made him wonder if it was a far bigger deal than he wanted to believe.

"Right. That's what I thought." Her lips curved into a smile again, but it didn't quite reach her eyes.

And as she reached for the little blue box and untied its white satin bow with trembling fingers, Anders almost believed he spied a hint of disappointment in her gaze.

Chapter Eight

"I need a favor." Chloe stood in the grand, glittering lobby of her brother's hotel and cut right to the chase.

Zander was a busy man, and she'd dropped by the Bennington without an appointment. Mercifully, he'd been free to see her.

He stood beneath the massive gold clock hanging from the ceiling, looking at her with unabashed amusement flickering in his gaze. "Does this have anything to do with your sudden, high-profile engagement?"

Of course he knew about Anders. The entire city did. "It does, actually."

"So it's true?" His eyebrows crept closer to his hairline. "Since Celestia Lane broke the story, I took it with a grain of salt. You're really getting married."

Zander glanced at her hand, where the Tiffany diamond on her ring finger sparkled as brightly as the Christmas tree at Rockefeller Center.

She'd come straight to the Bennington from Soho House, which meant she'd been wearing it for less than an hour. During the short ride from the restaurant, she kept stealing glances at it. Her engagement might have been fake, but the ring was the most beautiful piece of jewelry she'd ever seen. She realized she was absently caressing the band with the pad of her thumb, just as a real bride-to-be might do.

It needs to look real.

Mission accomplished. But should it *feel* as real as it did?

"Yes, I am." She cleared her throat. "I mean *we*. We're getting married—Anders and me."

So much for being believable.

"I see." His gaze narrowed. "Should I go into big-brother mode and ask if this is what you really want, or would you rather I keep my mouth shut and be supportive?"

She shot him a hopeful smile. "The latter, please."

He nodded. "Okay…"

"And if you could put in a good word with Mom, I'd really appreciate it." She couldn't face Emily. Chloe knew her mother, and the best way to handle her when she was upset was to give her some time and space.

Zander sighed. "How about a drink while we discuss these multiple favors I'm doing for you?"

Chloe never drank in the middle of the day, and

she'd just had a glass of wine with Anders. On any given afternoon in December, Chloe was usually wearing tap shoes and running on nothing but protein bars and adrenaline. But the sommelier at the Bennington was their cousin-in-law Evangeline Wilde and her taste in wine was legendary.

"Sounds good," Chloe said.

Thirty minutes and an incredible glass of vintage Chambertin Grand Cru later, she nodded as Zander went over the list they'd made on a Bennington notepad while sitting at the bar.

"You want a cake, a dozen or so bottles of Dom Perignon, music, an officiant..." He jotted something down. "What else am I missing?"

"Oh, flowers! Lolly will make an adorable flower girl."

"Flowers. Got it." He made another notation on the pad.

Couples got married at the Bennington all the time. As soon as Anders had mentioned having a real wedding ceremony, she'd hoped Zander could throw something together. And now he'd promised he would—no questions asked. If there was such thing as a brother-of-the-year award, he'd have a lock on it.

"I'll make sure we've got a basket of petals for her to toss, plus a bridal bouquet. Both ballrooms are already decked out in Christmas decorations, so we probably don't need anything else, flower-wise. We haven't even talked about when this is happening, although something tells me it's soon." He glanced up, and Chloe smiled back at him.

"*Really* soon. The sooner the better, actually," she said. "How about tomorrow?"

"Tomorrow." He blinked. "We might need to open another bottle of wine."

They did, and as she sipped, Zander assured her he could put something festive and intimate together. He'd even send out email invitations with the Bennington crest to Anders's business associates.

"A Christmas wedding it is, then," he said.

Chloe gave him a quiet smile.

A holiday wedding sounded dreamy. Christmas had always been her favorite time of year, and she couldn't imagine anything as beautiful and moving as exchanging vows beneath a bough of evergreen and twinkle lights on a snowy December evening. She'd wear a sprig of mistletoe tucked into her upswept hair, and a string quartet would play a winsome Christmas song as she walked down the aisle toward her handsome groom.

Except Anders wasn't really her groom. It would all be pretend—just another holiday performance.

A lump formed in her throat for some silly reason. She dug her fingernails into her palm.

Get it together. You chose this.

Yes, she had. And she had no regrets. She was doing the right thing—a *good* thing. The dazzling engagement ring on her hand was messing with her head. That was all.

"A Christmas wedding sounds perfect." Her lips trembled, as if the smile might wobble off her face. "It's every girl's dream come true."

"Then I think we should toast on it." Zander's face split into a wide grin and he held up his glass. "Cheers to the happy couple."

"Cheers." And as Chloe clinked her wineglass against his, toasting to Anders and the fulfillment of her girlish hopes and dreams, she could hear a little voice in the back of her head. Whispering, warning…

Be careful what you wish for.

"You really didn't have to reserve a room for me." Chloe clutched her garment bag to her chest as Zander led her into the Bennington's lavish bridal suite the following afternoon. "I just needed someplace to get dressed. I never expected…" Her throat clogged as she took in the four-poster bed, the glittering crystal chandelier and the robin's egg spun-silk walls—something blue. "…this."

She felt like she was standing in Marie Antoinette's bedroom. There was even a plate of pastel-colored macarons on the dressing table, and beside it, a silver ice bucket engraved with the Bennington's logo cradled a bottle of champagne.

Somehow she doubted the room was dog-friendly, even though Prancer's head poked out of the bag slung over her shoulder. But she needed the puppy here with her for moral support. Other than Anders, the little Yorkie was the only living soul who knew the truth about what she was about to do.

"I know I didn't have to, but I wanted to." Zander wrapped an arm around her shoulders and gave her a squeeze. "You're my baby sister, and today is your wedding day. It's special."

Not quite as special as you think it is. "Thank you, but I'm not exactly a baby anymore."

"You'll always be my baby sister, though." He winked. "I hope your groom realizes that."

Chloe swallowed. Her brother would pummel Anders if he knew the truth. And then he'd probably lock her in this exquisite room and throw away the key so she wouldn't be able to go through with the wedding.

"He's a good man, Zander." Finally, she'd managed to say something truthful.

"I believe you. He must be, if you chose him." Zander pushed back the cuff of his dress shirt and checked his watch. "And he should be waiting downstairs right about now."

She tossed her garment bag and pet carrier onto the bed. Prancer wiggled out of it and pawed at the silk duvet cover.

Zander didn't bat an eye. His imaginary brother-of-the-year trophy was getting bigger by the minute.

"Great. I'll go down and introduce you," she said.

"Not so fast." He wagged a finger at her. "I've got a room reserved for him, too. We're doing this right. The groom can't see the bride before the wedding."

She jammed her hands on her hips. "Are you kidding me? That's a silly superstition. You of all people shouldn't believe in stuff like that."

Had the rumor about the Bennington's runaway bride curse taught him nothing?

Zander shrugged. "Like I said, you're my baby

sister. It's tradition, and I don't want to risk any bad luck. You and Anders want to have a long and happy marriage, don't you?"

His right eyebrow shot up.

How about until just after Christmas? Would that be considered long?

Chloe forced a smile. "Of course we do."

"Then you're staying put. I'll deal with Anders. I haven't even met him yet. This will be good. It will give me a chance to get to know the man who's managed to sweep you off of your feet." He grinned, and something about the way he looked at her made the breath clog in her throat.

This was so much harder than she thought it would be—not the getting married part, but all the lies. She would have thought she'd be an expert at it by now, but lying to her family was beginning to get to her. They thought this was real. They thought she'd spend the rest of her life with Anders. They thought he'd be by her side on Christmas morning at the Wilde family brownstone, unwrapping gifts and sipping hot chocolate for years and years to come.

She took a deep breath and tried her best not to imagine what such a Christmas would be like, but images spun through her consciousness like snowflakes—Lolly setting out cookies for Santa Claus, Prancer tangled in the garland from the Christmas tree, Anders kissing her beneath the mistletoe.

God, what was wrong with her?

None of that would ever happen. They were pretending. It was just that the lie was so much more tempting to believe when her family was acting like she was living out some beautiful holiday love story.

She swallowed, with great difficulty. The only thing worse than lying to her own flesh and blood would be having to beg them to lie on her behalf. She couldn't ask them to perjure themselves at Lolly's guardianship hearing. She wouldn't.

"Okay, I'm on my way down. I'll see you in an hour or so, when you're ready to walk down the aisle." Zander paused with his hand on the doorknob. "Give me a call if you need anything, but don't worry. Mom's on her way, and she's got a surprise for you."

Chloe's stomach tumbled. She still hadn't seen her mother face-to-face since Emily had flown into the dance school in a panic over the *Vows* column, and frankly, she was a little terrified of having to explain her sudden nuptials. Zander had assured her he'd calmed Emily down, but still. The last thing Chloe needed was a surprise. "Wait—what are you talking about?"

But her brother didn't respond. His grin widened and he closed the door behind him, leaving her alone.

"Well, then." Chloe sighed and glanced at Prancer. The little dog was rolling around on the large bed, rubbing her little face on all the pillows, oblivious to Chloe's existential crisis.

"You're no help," she muttered and reached for the ice-cold bottle of champagne.

She popped the cork and poured a glass. Liquid courage. It couldn't hurt, could it?

A knock sounded on the door. "Chloe, it's me."

Her mother.

Chloe set down her champagne flute. Maybe a clear head was a better idea. “Coming.”

She took a deep breath and opened the door, not altogether sure what to expect. Emily with her arms crossed and a look of profound disappointment on her face? Maybe even tears? *Please, no. Anything but that.*

Blessedly, she was greeted by neither of those nightmare scenarios. Emily stood smiling at the threshold, dressed to the nines in a floaty, mother-of-the-bride type dress and her hair in a fancy twist like she’d always worn back when she competed in ballroom dance competitions. She held a garment bag over her arm—a much longer one than the garment bag currently flung across the bed.

“Mom, you look gorgeous.” Chloe didn’t want to look at the garment bag, but she couldn’t take her eyes off it. She was equal parts curious and terrified of whatever was inside. It was awfully big, and Emily was already dressed for the wedding, which meant it could contain only one thing.

She held the door open wide. “Come in.”

Emily walked past her, while Prancer yipped and spun in excited circles on the bed.

“You brought the puppy?” Her mother laughed.

“Yes, I thought it might be fun for Lolly if Prancer was in the wedding.”

“That’s adorable.” Emily inhaled a deep breath. “Look at you, already thinking about her like she’s your daughter.”

Chloe felt oddly like she might fall apart, so she wrapped her arms around her middle to keep herself together. Were she and Anders doing the right thing? Lolly was the sole reason for the marriage, and now they were being forced to drag her into it. Were they doing more harm than good? "She's a precious little girl. Anders loves her very much."

"I know he does. They've both been through a lot." Emily held up her hand. "Don't worry. I'm not going to try and talk you out of this or even ask if you're sure. If marrying Anders is really and truly what you want, I'm here for you. We all are. This is your wedding day, a day for joy and love and happiness."

Relief coursed through Chloe, but it was short-lived, because then Emily held up the garment bag, the aforementioned surprise, just as Chloe feared.

"I brought you something." Tears shimmered in Emily's eyes.

"Is that a wedding gown?" Chloe's voice shook, and she gestured to the bed. "Because you really shouldn't have bought me anything. Maybe we can return it. This is supposed to be a simple ceremony, and I already had a white dress hanging in my closet. It will work."

She'd planned on wearing the same pleated chiffon number she'd worn to city hall when she and Anders had gotten the marriage license. It was perfectly fine, especially for a wedding that wasn't technically a wedding. Plus, she'd rather liked the way Anders had looked at her when she'd worn it, although that shouldn't have mattered a bit.

"Calm down." Her mother rolled her eyes. "I didn't spend any money."

She unzipped the garment bag, and a puff of white tulle spilled out. The gown was beautiful. It was also very familiar. Chloe had seen pictures of it in family albums and on the wall of the brownstone all her life. When she was a little girl, she'd dreamed of wearing it on her wedding day. Her mother had even let her try it on once when she was ten years old. It had nearly swallowed her whole, but being wrapped up in all that vintage tulle and lace had made her feel like a princess.

She squeezed her eyes shut tight as Lolly's words came rushing back to her.

Are you a Christmas princess?

She wasn't a princess. She wasn't even a Christmas bride. Not really.

She forced her eyes open and gave her mother a wobbly smile. "You want me to wear your wedding gown?"

"Of course I do, darling. You've always loved this dress." She took a step closer and cupped Chloe's cheek with her free hand. "If marrying Anders is what you want, then it's what I want, too. You'll wear it, won't you?"

She couldn't say no. If she did, it would be a huge red flag.

And her mother was right. Chloe had always pictured herself walking down the aisle in this very dress, only now that she thought about it, she'd never once imagined the man waiting for her at the end of the aisle would be Steven. But if he'd wanted to marry her, she would have said yes. Wouldn't she?

She twisted the ring on her finger—the one Anders had given her.

"I'd love to wear it." If Anders had taken a liking to her little white dress, his eyes would probably fall out of his head when she walked into the ballroom in this one.

Not that it mattered, except it would be nice if he looked at her with that glowy expression of adoration that grooms always had when they first saw their wives-to-be all decked out in bridal white. For her family's sake, obviously.

Liar.

Tears pricked her eyes. She'd been painfully aware of all the lies she'd been telling her family, but when had she started lying to herself?

"Do you think it will fit?" she said.

Maybe it wouldn't. Maybe it was like Cinderella's glass slipper and would fit only if fate willed it so.

Emily removed the dress fully from the bag. Age had changed its color from frosty white to a lovely, pale shade of blush, like a Valentine from days gone by or a timeless promise. Hundreds of tiny rhinestones scattered over the gown's full tulle skirt glittered in the soft light of the chandelier.

"Don't you worry, love." Emily pressed a hand to her heart. "Something tells me it will."

Chapter Nine

The kindness of the Wildes was beginning to make Anders wonder if he was about to make a mistake. The biggest one of his life, perhaps.

Her brother had greeted him in the lobby with a wide grin, clapped him on the back and said, "I'm Zander. Welcome to the family."

Anders had felt like the biggest, worst impostor in the world. But no, he'd soon realized things were just getting started. He could sink to new, much lower depths as the day progressed. Like when Allegra arrived on the scene with a special flower girl dress for Lolly, and Emily Wilde grew misty-eyed as she pinned a flower to the lapel of his tuxedo.

Grant had been right. He was a monster. He'd given little to no actual thought to what this charade would do to Chloe's family. They expected her to be married to him for the rest of her life. They thought he was going to be a permanent part of their family.

They thought he loved her.

And he didn't, obviously. The overwhelming tightness that he felt in his chest when he thought about her and the way he almost felt like everything was going to be okay when she was around couldn't be love. People didn't fall in love in a matter of days. It just wasn't possible.

What he felt for Chloe was gratitude. Without her, he wouldn't have a chance of securing Lolly's custody. She was saving his family. She was saving *him.*

And how was he returning the favor? By hurting the people who cared about her.

He looked around the Bennington ballroom, where rows of white chairs connected by swags of evergreen and frosted holly berries held his friends and colleagues. Chloe's sister, Tessa, her cousin Ryan and his wife, Evangeline, along with their newborn baby and Allegra, were all lined up in the front row. Emily Wilde was at the back of the room, helping Lolly with Prancer's leash and the basket of white rose petals she would scatter down the aisle. Someone had even fashioned a tiny ring pillow for the dog to wear on its back.

It was all so heartfelt, like a scene out of a Hallmark movie.

Come January, these people will despise me.

As well they should. He was already beginning to despise himself.

He needed to see Chloe or at least talk to her. He needed her to remind him that she was fine with all this, that they were doing the right thing. He reached into the pocket of his tux for his cell phone, and as he dialed her number, he couldn't help but wonder when he'd started to rely on her so much. Because he had. He *needed* her, and not just for Lolly's sake.

Anders wasn't accustomed to needing someone. *Any*one. He'd been on his own since he was seventeen years old, with no one but Grant to rely on. And now Grant was gone, too. Sometimes he wondered what he'd done to deserve such a lonely life. What had prompted fate to be so cruel as to take their parents away when they were practically still kids, and then take Grant and Olivia in the same sudden manner a decade and a half later?

Then Anders would remember there was no such thing as fate. Nor was his life lonely. He'd been doing just fine, until lately. But soon he'd be fine again, as would Lolly. He just needed to get through today, and he definitely needed to stop thinking about things like fate and destiny. They were nothing but myths, just like love at first sight.

A vision of Chloe dressed in her silly reindeer costume and glaring at him as she accused him of being a puppy thief on the day they'd first met flashed in his mind.

His grip on his cell phone tightened. The call rolled to voice mail and Chloe's honeyed voice came through on the recording, and he sighed.

"It's time, man." A hand landed on his shoulder.

Anders looked up. Zander. “Now?”

“Now.” Zander grinned and nodded toward the tower of white poinsettias, covered in twinkle lights and shaped like a massive Christmas tree, where a clergyman stood, waiting to make Anders a married man. “Are you ready to become my brother-in-law?”

Are you ready to make Chloe your wife?

Anders nodded. “I am.”

The next few moments passed in a blur as he took his place beside the minister, the last of the guests filled the seats and music filled the air. A white grand piano had been brought in, where Julian Shine, Chloe’s brother-in-law, played a gentle Christmas carol with just a touch of jazzy flair. Anders’s chest had that terrible, tightly wound feeling again as Lolly came toward him up the aisle, dropping rose petals as she went. The silly dog tugged at the end of her leash, causing the ring pillow to slide around to her belly, and all the guests laughed.

Somehow it made him feel like more of a monster than ever.

This is wrong.

Then Chloe appeared, walking toward him on the arm of her brother, looking like something out of a dream. Only not the sort of dreams that he’d been having lately—nightmares that caused him to wake in a cold sweat, panicked at the thought of losing Lolly, of disappointing Grant again. Permanently.

This was a different kind of dream. The kind where a woman with laughter as sparkling as the summer sun high in the sky over Central Park wanted to promise to love, honor and cherish him for the rest of his life. The kind of dream where he'd gotten into an argument with a beautiful woman over a silly little dog, and now that woman wore his ring.

"Hi," she said, snapping him out of his trance when she came to a stop alongside him.

Zander gave him a look that somehow felt like both a warning and a blessing at the same time, before taking his seat. Chloe passed a bouquet of blue spruce and mistletoe to Lolly, who cradled it in her arms like a priceless treasure and sat down beside Emily Wilde.

Then it was just the two of them, hand in hand, as the minister talked about love and commitment and the meaning of forever. And by God, if this wasn't what a real wedding felt like, Anders didn't know what did.

The minister turned toward Chloe. "Do you, Chloe Wilde, take Anders Kent, to have and to hold, from this day forward, for better, for worse, for richer, for poorer, in sickness and in health, until death do you part?"

She looked up at Anders, and her eyes went misty. *Don't cry. Please don't.* He didn't know what those unshed tears meant—he only knew that he wouldn't be able to go through with it if she had even a trace of doubt about what they were doing.

"Are you sure about this?" he whispered. "It's okay if you're not. I'll find another way. I promise."

He didn't care if the minister heard him. He didn't

care that the promise he'd just made was probably an empty one. He was running out of time.

Chloe smiled through her tears and she gripped his hand as if it were a lifeline. As if she wasn't just saving him, but they were somehow saving each other.

Then she turned to the minister and said, "I do."

It was over so quickly.

One moment, Chloe was walking down the aisle toward Anders with her heart beating wildly in her chest as he looked at her like she was a real bride and he was a real groom and this was a real wedding—the wedding of their dreams.

And then in a flash, there was a shiny new wedding band on her finger, right beside the diamond Anders had given her the day before, and the minister was smiling at them and saying, "Anders and Chloe have vowed, in our presence, to be loyal and loving toward each other. They have formalized the existence of the bond between them with words spoken and with the giving and receiving of rings."

Bond…they were bonded together. She and Anders Kent, who she'd met less than a week ago.

The clergyman's smile grew wider. "Therefore, it is my pleasure to now pronounce them husband and wife."

A forbidden thrill coursed through Chloe. Or was it just nerves? Right, that was what it was—nerves. She was going to have to kiss Anders now, right there in front of all her friends and family. *For the very first time.*

How on earth had she forgotten about the kiss? They should have practiced first, at least one time. First kisses were almost always awkward. She never knew which way to tilt her head, and they usually went on far too long, as if neither party wanted to be the first to pull away, even after they'd both begun to suffocate from lack of oxygen.

The odds of pulling this off and making it look natural were slim to none, but they didn't exactly have a choice. Regular newlyweds wouldn't exactly take a pass on their first kiss as a married couple.

She held her breath and waited for the minister to say it.

"Anders, you may now kiss your bride."

His bride.

His bride.

His.

Chloe's knees went a little weak as she lifted her gaze to Anders, peeking up at him through the thick fringe of her lashes. Right before she'd said her vows, he'd given her an out. He'd stopped looking at her as if she were a bride, and for a tentative sliver of a moment, he'd regarded her as something else—not quite a stranger, but not as a loved one, either. Not even a pretend loved one. But instead, more like someone he was destined to disappoint.

The moment had passed after she said "I do," and now he was watching her in a way that no one ever had before. Not Steven. Not the boy whose lips first touched hers all those years ago at the ballet school while they danced *Romeo and Juliet.* No man who'd kissed her had ever gazed at her with such hunger in his eyes. Such need, such blatant desire, like he wasn't about to kiss her, but to devour her whole.

It was almost frightening. Or rather, it should have been, considering it was a fake kiss to seal a fake marriage to her fake husband.

But as she draped her arms around his neck and lifted her mouth toward his—straining, seeking—she realized the fire skittering along her skin wasn't a sign of apprehension. It was pure anticipation. Pure longing. The exact sort of longing she saw looking back at her in Anders's moody blue eyes.

I am in so much trouble.

It was her final thought as her eyes fluttered closed in the excruciating moment before his mouth came down on hers—a moment that seemed to shimmer with promise, despite the ridiculousness of their situation. She wondered if he felt it, too, or if she was alone in the realization that this was a dangerous game they were playing, that it seemed impossible one of them wouldn't walk away from their union in the days following Christmas and face the New Year with a heart in tatters.

She wasn't alone. She could tell by the naked vulnerability in the tender way he touched her, so uncharacteristic for a man like Anders. A strong man. A careful one. The kind of man who put his faith in words on a page instead of in people. But there was no trace of that brand of detachment in the first brush of his lips. It was as forgotten as the contract he couldn't seem to remember to have her sign. Instead, there was want and heat and a feeling so flush with desperation that her eyes filled with tears again. This time, they were too numerous to blink away. They flowed down her cheeks as she opened for him, letting him consume her…taking him in.

Bonded together.

The words echoed in her consciousness, her heart pounding in time with the sentiment.

That was what this was. More than a kiss, more than her mouth seeking his. This was a bond. A promise. A vow. *I do.* The words still lingered on his tongue as it slid against hers, so decadently sweet. And beyond the something borrowed and something blue, the kiss was another thing, too. It was an invitation engraved upon her heart. A question.

Do you want me?

Her fingertips tightened around the smooth collar of his tuxedo jacket as his hands slid up the back of her dress, burning her skin through the delicate lace covering her shoulder blades.

I do, I do, I do.

Somewhere in the periphery, a throat cleared. Chloe wasn't sure who it belonged to. She wasn't even sure how she'd managed to stay upright for the duration of that kiss, which somehow seemed to have lasted both a split second and an eternity.

Anders pulled back and rested his forehead against hers, his eyes twinkling with sapphire light.

"What was that?" she choked.

He brushed the pad of his thumb against her lower lip, where all the nerve endings in her body had gathered into one delicious place. And then he smiled. "That, my darling bride, was a kiss."

It was done.

The overwhelming sense of relief Anders expected to feel once the vows had been exchanged and the minister handed over the certificate of marriage never came. Instead, his heart brimmed with an emotion that felt suspiciously like joy as the short and simple ceremony gave way to a wedding reception. A party.

And why shouldn't he feel happy at a party? Wasn't that what parties were for?

Yet, as he shook hands with the partners from his office and accepted their congratulations, he couldn't seem to let go of Chloe's fingertips. Again, he told himself that was normal. Just part of the act. But he kept finding himself toying with the diamond on her finger, checking to make sure it was still there, that this day had actually been real.

And through it all—through the first dance and the cutting of the cake and the toast from Chloe's brother that made an unprecedented lump lodge in his throat—he couldn't shake the memory of the kiss.

It had rocked him to the core, that kiss.

If they hadn't been standing inches away from a clergyman, in full view of all of Chloe's nearest and dearest, he never would have ended it. If he hadn't made a solemn promise to himself, and to Chloe, not to touch her, he'd be upstairs right now in one of the Bennington's sumptuous king-size beds, tasting her again. Touching her…

Every tempting inch of her balletic body.

That couldn't happen, obviously. But Anders was suddenly excruciatingly aware of the fact that they'd be sharing a bedroom for the next few weeks. By Manhattan standards, his apartment was massive. It had a panoramic view of Central Park, lush with cherry blossoms in the springtime and frosted with whirling snowflakes and Christmas spirit during the winter. But the vast majority of its square footage was taken up by the expansive living room and its floor-to-ceiling windows. He had a grand total of two bedrooms, which had always been double the amount he actually needed.

Until he'd become a family man overnight.

Mrs. Summers had helped him transform the spare bedroom into a room for Lolly. It was more of an oasis than a bedroom, like a little girl's sparkly, pink fantasy-come-true, with a canopy bed and glow-in-the-dark stars on the ceiling. Which left the master bedroom to Anders, just like always.

Except now, Chloe would be coming home with him, and he couldn't very well ask her to sleep on the sofa. He would have gladly made himself at home on the living room couch, but he wondered what kind of example that set for Lolly. At the very least, it would prompt questions. Grant and Olivia had always been affectionate with one another. He couldn't see Grant spending many nights sleeping on the sofa.

But as it turned out, they wouldn't have to deal with the awkward matter of sleeping arrangements at his apartment. Not quite yet, because when the wedding reception wound down to a close and the purple New York twilight deepened to a velvety, inky blue, the Christmas shoppers lining the bustling sidewalks of Park Avenue found their way home and Zander Wilde tucked a card key into the inside pocket of Anders's tuxedo jacket.

"The honeymoon suite," he said, handing Anders yet another glass of sparkling champagne. "It's yours for the night. My treat."

"I can't accept," Anders protested, as visions of a heart-shaped bed and a bathtub built for two danced in his head.

Not likely, considering the Bennington was a five-star hotel. Still, even without the stereotypical romantic trappings, he wouldn't last five minutes in a honeymoon suite with Chloe. Not after that kiss.

"Don't be ridiculous. Of course you can. I own this hotel, remember? And you're family now." Zander's gaze narrowed. "Just promise me one thing."

Anders's jaw clenched. "What's that?"

"Keep making my sister happy. I've never seen Chloe glowing like she is today." Zander gave his chest a pat, right where the key to the honeymoon suite rested against his heart. "Don't worry about a thing. Julian and Tessa are taking Lolly and Prancer until tomorrow morning. Wild horses couldn't keep your niece away. Tessa is a principal dancer at the Manhattan Ballet, and she's promised Lolly a serious dress-up session in some of her old costumes. Let's all meet on the top floor for brunch tomorrow at Bennington 8."

Then he was gone, and Anders could only stand there with the key to the honeymoon suite in his pocket like a lead weight as he watched Chloe hugging her family members goodbye just feet away.

He wanted her. No question. He wanted her so badly that he couldn't stop thinking about all the things he longed to do to her in that lavish hotel suite. Most of all, he wanted to kiss her again. He needed it, just to see if the first time had been a fluke. Surely it was just the product of their unique circumstances. The past few days had been a wild ride, and he was running on some crazy mixture of loss and adrenaline. His mind and body were playing tricks on him, making him believe ever so slightly in the fairy tale they'd concocted.

Deep down, he knew he was fooling himself. It didn't matter why he wanted to kiss Chloe again or why he wanted to unfasten that delicate confection of a dress she was wearing and watch it fall into a pile of fluff at her feet. He just did. He wanted it with every broken part of his soul.

But Zander's words echoed in his head.

Keep making my sister happy.

They reminded him all too much of who he was, what he was—a monster, according to his own flesh and blood.

No sex. He'd made her a promise, and he intended to keep it.

Chapter Ten

"Wow, can you believe this room?" Chloe spun in a slow circle, taking in the pale gold paneled walls, the creamy white crown molding—as abundant and extravagant as icing on a wedding cake—and what had to be the most massive bed she'd ever set eyes on. The honeymoon suite. *Oh God.* "I mean, have you ever seen anything like this?"

She attempted a light and carefree laugh, but it came out strained. Forced. "What am I saying? Of course you have."

Stop. Talking. What was wrong with her? She'd been babbling nonstop since they'd crossed the threshold. There was no telling what kind of nonsense would come out of her mouth next.

Anders folded his arms across his chest and gazed

impassively at her. "Why would you think I'd spent any time whatsoever in a honeymoon suite before?"

"I don't." She shook her head. "I just meant you're probably used to nice surroundings. Sorry, I'm not sure what I'm even saying. I'm just..."

"Nervous?" He arched a brow in amusement.

"Yes, actually." She released a breath she hadn't realized she'd been holding. "I am."

"Don't be. You can relax." He unbuttoned his tuxedo jacket, slipped out of it and tossed it onto the opulent silk sofa in the suite's luxe sitting area. Then he walked toward her and gave her a little tap on the nose. "There's nothing to be nervous about, love. I made you a promise, remember?"

She swallowed. "Of course I remember."

No sex.

Whose terrible idea had that been? Oh yeah, hers.

He gave her a tight smile, raked his hand in his hair and meandered back to the sofa as if he didn't have a care in the world.

Seriously?

Chloe was suddenly livid—livid at Anders for kissing her like he had and livid at herself for liking it so much. She'd thought it had meant something. She wasn't sure what, exactly, but she knew it didn't involve Anders sleeping on the couch.

She stared daggers at him as he kicked off his shoes. His eyes narrowed, and then the corner of his mouth lifted into a half grin. Moving as slowly as possible, with the languid grace of some kind of predatory animal, he reached for one of the French cuffs of his shirt and unfastened the cuff link. Without tearing his gaze from hers, he dropped it into a little tray on the table beside the couch. It pierced the strained silence with a tiny clang. Platinum on china.

Chloe's face burned, but she didn't dare fan herself. If he could be happy sleeping on the sofa, she could be just as unaffected by his billionaire bachelor striptease. Except he wasn't a bachelor anymore, was he?

He was hers.

Sort of.

"You might want to turn around." He unfastened his other cuff link, slid his bow tie off and undid the top button of his immaculate white shirt. His fingertips paused at the next button down. Then his half grin morphed into a wide smile, with a touch of smolder for good measure. To her complete and utter mortification, he made a little spinning motion with one of his pointer fingers.

Two could play at that game.

Obediently, she turned around to face the wall. Then she ran her fingers through her hair and twirled it into a high bun, so her new husband-who-wasn't-really-her-husband could have a clear, unobstructed view of her back. A lifetime of being a dancer meant she could secure a ballerina bun with nothing but a twist of her wrist. She spent more time than necessary tucking the loose waves into place and then slid the tips of her fingers lazily down the side of her neck.

She knew he was watching her, even before she heard his sharp intake of breath. She could feel the heat of his gaze, as warm and sultry as a hot summer day. It felt like tiny little fires breaking out all over her skin, and it made her want him even more, if such a thing was possible. What was it about him that made her feel this way? So adored…so *seen,* when he'd never so much as touched her. He'd kissed her once, only because he had to, and she was a goner. It defied logic.

Deep down, though, she knew why. She wasn't a prop to Anders. She was a person. He knew all about her toy soldier fiasco, and he didn't care. He saw her and he *wanted* her, purely for who she was.

A tiny voice sounded in the back of her head, so tiny she almost didn't recognize it as her own. *Isn't this all supposed to be pretend?*

She pushed it away. There was nothing make-believe about the pounding of her pulse, nor was it an illusion when she reached behind her neck and unclasped the fastening of her dress. Only one thought spun through her mind as she paused and let the gown fall away, pooling at her feet in a whisper of dreams and lace. *This….* this…*is real.*

"Are you sure about this?" Anders's breath was hot on the back of her neck. She wasn't sure how long he'd been standing there, or when he'd gotten up from the couch. All that mattered was that he had.

She peered at him over her bare shoulder. "That's the second time you've asked me that question today, Mr. Kent."

"And?" His eyes were unfathomably dark—darker

than she'd ever seen them. Glittering pools of indigo blue. "What's your answer, Mrs. Kent?"

Dressed now in nothing but her lacy panties and her wedding rings, she turned to face the gloriously handsome man who was now her husband.

"The same as before." The same as it had been since that very first day at the animal shelter, whether or not she wanted to admit it. "Yes, please."

He kissed her, and it was a different kind of kiss than the wild, untamed one that had sealed their vows. This kiss was slow and reverent—tender in a way that made her insides flutter, even as her body went molten.

Her hands slid over his crisp white tuxedo shirt, and she became excruciatingly aware of the fact that he was still dressed while she was almost entirely naked. If she'd been with someone else, she might have been embarrassed. But with Anders, she didn't feel an ounce of shame, nor a bit of the awkwardness that she'd always experienced with a new lover. She hoped it wasn't because Anders was her husband, since that would mean the lovely wedding and the romantic vows had gone straight to her head, when she knew better than to let that happen.

This man whose hands were now cupping her breasts, and whose mouth was making a decadent trail of kisses along the curve of her neck, wasn't her soul mate. He wasn't the love of her life, no matter how good it felt when he touched her or how quickened her breath became when his lips dipped lower and his tongue brushed softly against her nipple.

But the words they'd said to one another in front of their families and friends were heavy with meaning. They were the most intimate words of all, and whether she and Anders had meant them or not, it was as if their bodies had heard those words.

His hands slid to her waist, fingertips brushing lightly, gingerly, against her skin.

To have and to hold.

He dropped to his knees, his mouth moving lower, and lower still, until her panties were on the floor and he parted her thighs ever so gently, pressing a hot, openmouthed kiss between her legs.

To love and to cherish.

Her head fell backward, and in the moment before she shattered, a sound came out of her mouth that she'd never heard herself make before. It was as if she'd become another person entirely—Chloe Wilde had ceased to exist and Chloe Kent, wild and romantic, had taken her place.

Till death do us part.

Anders carried Chloe to the bed and she mewed like a kitten into the crook of his neck. The cat who'd gotten the cream.

"Easy, love. We're just getting started," he murmured into her hair.

They had all night—a night to explore one another, to learn all the little ways to give each other pleasure. He wanted to know all of them. He wanted to memorize every inch of her balletic body and kiss every tantalizing curve. He needed to know her, *really* know her…this ethereal beauty of a woman who now shared his name.

He placed her gently on the smooth silk sheets and started to undress, but then paused, unable to move a muscle as he looked down at his wife, bare and beautiful. He couldn't take his eyes off her, and he wondered if it would always be like this…if looking at her would forever make him ache with need, if touching her porcelain skin would fill him with an emotion he couldn't name, one that almost made him forget that they weren't really man and wife. They were still just pretending.

He slid out of his clothes, and as she reached for him, the diamond on her finger shimmered in the darkness. He watched, mesmerized, as her elegant hand closed around his erection, making him moan.

With this ring, I thee wed.

His breath came hard and quick, and he tried to slow it down, to make himself last. As good as she made him feel, he didn't want to finish like this. He needed her legs wrapped around his waist. He needed to cover her willowy body with his.

He needed to be inside her.

For as long as we both shall live.

"I want you, Chloe," he growled, winding a lock of her hair around his finger, pushing it back from her face so he could look her in the eyes.

They'd gone liquid with desire, dark and heavy-lidded. Bedroom eyes. But he and Chloe had an agreement, and they were about to cross every last line they'd previously drawn in the sand. He wanted her to be sure, because if she wasn't, they'd stop right now. It wouldn't be easy, but he'd manage.

"Tell me you want me, love." He kissed her, and her lips tasted sugary sweet, like wedding cake and fizzy champagne. "I need to hear you say it."

"I want you, Anders." She nipped gently at his bottom lip, and he nearly came. It was a miracle that he hadn't already. "Desperately so."

No woman had ever made him feel this way before—half out of his mind with need. Something strange was happening, something that felt far more meaningful than it should have, but he didn't want to stop and analyze it. He'd been doing just that his entire life, and where had it gotten him?

Dumb luck had led him to Chloe Wilde. He didn't deserve her, and he'd never been quite so keenly aware of that fact as he was now, poised above her, ready to slide into her warm, perfect body.

Chloe reached for him again, guiding him to her entrance. He took a deep breath and pushed inside, pausing to give her a chance to adjust. Then, as he kissed her, she opened for him and he thrust his way home.

And two shall become one.

Chapter Eleven

What had they done?

Chloe had insisted on only one rule: keeping things platonic. Everyone knew what platonic meant. It was no big mystery. Platonic meant no kissing, no cuddling and absolutely no sex. Yet here she was, less than twelve hours after marrying Anders Kent, waking up naked in bed beside him.

Or more accurately, on top of him.

Oh God.

She slid off him and wrapped the sheet around herself, moving as gingerly as possible. She was afraid to slide out of the bed in case the movement woke him. The minute he was conscious, they needed to talk about the enormous mistake they'd just made. They needed to set new boundaries, reinstate the strict no-sex policy.

Chloe wasn't quite ready to have that conversation. Not while she was feeling so pleasantly warm and sated, wearing nothing but a Tiffany diamond.

Which your new husband had been contractually obligated to give you.

How could she have been so stupid? She'd somehow managed to convince herself that the kiss at the wedding had meant something when it so obviously did not. Otherwise, she wouldn't have had to tempt him into sleeping with her. He would have been an active and willing participant from the second they'd walked into the honeymoon suite.

She glanced down at him, sleeping so soundly beside her. Funny, she could have sworn he'd once told her he never slept past five in the morning. Yet it had to be at least eight o'clock. The bedsheets were bathed in a pink glow from the morning sun's rays glinting off the surrounding skyscrapers. They'd never managed to close the velvet drapes before they'd fallen into bed. From the moment he'd put his hands on her, everything had become a blur of shimmering heat. Of sensation. Her mother's wedding gown was still in a pile on the floor, as if she'd stepped out of it only moments ago. The various parts of Anders's tuxedo littered the sitting area, from one end of the room to the other.

She bit back a smile. *This is what a real honeymoon suite looks like the morning after a wedding.*

Then she blinked. What was wrong with her? This

was exactly what she'd been afraid of in that pivotal moment before Anders kissed her for the first time. She'd known she was in trouble. She'd sensed it as surely as she'd sensed the epic domino effect she'd set into motion when she'd stumbled during the toy soldier number in the Thanksgiving parade. Only then, the destruction had played out in slow motion. She'd watched, consciously aware of each wrong move, every tiny misstep, as one dancer after another fell to the ground.

Not this time. This time, she'd plunged headfirst into disaster. *Intentionally.* She'd known exactly what she was doing, from the minute he'd taken her hand and led her away from the ballroom. He hadn't seduced her as she'd expected him to, but no problem. She'd taken matters into her own hands.

This was how she'd end up with a broken heart. She wasn't the type of person who could indulge in meaningless sex. She wished she could. Oh, how she wished it, but she just wasn't wired that way. The whole fake marriage idea might have worked if she'd stuck to the rules, but now she wasn't so sure.

Could she really walk away from Anders and Lolly in less than a month?

You don't have a choice. You have to.

She glanced down at her temporary husband. His chest rose and fell with the languid grace of a dreamer, and the sternness in his features seemed softer somehow. More relaxed.

He looks happy. She swallowed hard around the

knot in her throat. He looked happier than she'd ever seen him.

But what did she know? She was Anders's wife, but she'd known him for less than a week.

His eyes drifted open, first one and then the other, and then his mouth curved into a tender smile as he realized she'd been watching him sleep. Her heart clenched. *It's too late*, she thought. She was already in too deep. The thought of losing this, of losing *him*, already left her with a cavernous, hollow feeling in her heart.

This is why people shouldn't sleep with their pretend husbands.

She bit her bottom lip to keep it from quivering.

"Hey." Anders's brow furrowed and he slipped his hand beneath the sheet to cup her breast and run his thumb gently over her nipple. "Why do I get the feeling you're about to climb out of bed?"

Because I am. His touch drew a sigh out of her. Just one tender brush of his fingertips—that was all it took for her body to crave him again. She could feel it building inside. The want. The need.

"We have brunch, remember?" She forced herself to crawl away from him while she still could, and nearly tumbled to the floor in a tangle of sheets and desperation.

Over twenty years of dance classes and she couldn't even manage to get out of bed gracefully. Perfect.

She righted herself and pulled the sheet tighter around her bare body, consciously aware of the deepening frown on Anders's perfectly chiseled face. When at last she'd become steady on her feet, she flashed him a smile. A fake one, obviously, since pretending was all she knew how to do now.

He didn't move a muscle. He just stared at her as she silently willed her heart to close itself up like a book that could be read only one time and then tucked away and forgotten.

His gaze slid to the clock on the nightstand and then back to her. Was it her imagination or did her heart actually hurt when he looked at her now? *You have no one to blame but yourself.*

He'd asked her. More than once.

Are you sure?

Tell me you want me... I need to hear you say it.

She'd been sure. She'd never been so sure about anything in her life, never wanted anything as badly as she wanted him inside her. And that was precisely the problem.

"Brunch isn't for almost three hours." His voice was raw and delicious. It sounded like pure sex.

A rebellious shiver coursed through Chloe. This conversation would have been so much easier if he weren't naked.

Anders stood and closed the distance between them, and she couldn't force herself to look away from his long, lean body and its sculpted planes as he moved toward her.

She'd kissed those muscles. She'd dug her fingernails into that glorious flesh as he'd pushed his way inside her. In the mirror behind him, she could see little half-moon marks on his back—evidence of her longing, her passion. Passion that no man had ever brought out of her before. Only him. Only Anders.

What did it mean? What did *any of this* mean?

"Talk to me, love." He reached for her hand, then gingerly lifted it to his mouth and kissed the place where her wedding ring wrapped around her finger. "Tell me what's going on."

There was no way she could do this for two more weeks, not if he expected her to pack up her things and leave on Christmas Eve.

"Nothing." She pulled her hand away, pretending not to notice the angry knot in his jaw as she did so. "It's just that the wedding is over now."

"And?" His gaze narrowed, and he peered at her as if daring her to continue.

She didn't have to. It wasn't too late to throw herself into his arms and kiss him, to start the morning over again. But if she did, what would happen the next morning? And the one after that?

What would happen when she woke up the day after Lolly's custody hearing and remembered everything had been for show?

"And last night was wonderful, but it should probably be a onetime thing." She stopped talking before she choked on a sob.

Out of the many, many lies she'd told in the past few weeks, this one was the biggest. It was the most devastating whopper of them all. She didn't want it to be a onetime thing. She wanted it to be more than that. She might even want it to be forever.

For as long as we both shall live.

What was she thinking? She still didn't know her husband. Not really. He'd just sexed the sense right out of her, which was yet another reason they shouldn't sleep together again. Ever.

Anders didn't say anything. He just stood there, studying her, as if he was trying to see inside her head.

Thank goodness he couldn't. They'd been married all of five minutes and she'd gone and reversed the script. But he didn't need to know that, did he? "I mean, that's what we agree on. Right?"

Say something.

If only he'd give her some indication that he felt the same way. One word…that was all it would take. But she couldn't just put herself out there if he didn't feel the same way. They'd agreed on a fake marriage. He'd even wanted her to sign a contract.

She peered up at him, breathless, willing him to argue with her. For a bittersweet second, she thought he might. In the morning light, his eyes were bluer than ever, as clear as the sparkling sea. And an invisible force seemed to pull her toward him, inviting her to dive right in.

But then he blinked, and it was gone. Whatever magical connection or genuine bond that had formed between them when they'd said *I do* fell away, and his expression hardened into stone.

Right before her eyes, he seemed to change from the man she'd spent the night with back into the brooding stranger she'd met at the animal shelter.

Anders was in no mood for brunch.

He wasn't sure how he could sip mimosas with

the Wildes over French toast and gourmet waffles when he was still trying to unravel whatever had gone wrong the night before. Because something had *definitely* happened. He just wasn't sure what it was.

But he showed up and did his damnedest to smile and make small talk with Chloe and her family, because that was what husbands did, right? And Anders was Chloe's husband now. She was his *wife*.

In name only. He took a bitter gulp of black coffee.

Why did the businesslike nature of their union grate so much? He'd known what he was getting into. They both had. There'd been no ambiguity about the rules—a platonic relationship, no sex. They'd never sworn not to have feelings for one another, but that had been a given. And now here he was, sitting beside Chloe the morning after their wedding, wanting nothing more than to reach for her hand under the table or brush the hair from her face and kiss her full on the lips for all the world to see.

Lolly wiggled her way between them, gripping Tessa's cell phone and chattering about her sleepover at Tessa and Julian's apartment. "And after we watched a dance movie, Tessa let me try on some of her costumes. We took pictures. Look!"

Chloe helped her scroll through images on the iPhone, and as adorable as they were, the nagging sense of regret in Anders's gut grew worse as he looked at them.

"I'm glad you had fun, sweetheart." He kissed the top of Lolly's head, careful to avoid the perfect ballerina bun Tessa had created for her.

"She's welcome anytime," Julian said, signing the words at the same time, since Tessa was deaf.

The whole family seemed to know American Sign Language, something he hadn't realized the day before during the busy buildup to the wedding. Lolly had apparently picked up a few basics during her sleepover, because when Anders reminded her to thank Tessa and Julian, she'd pressed her fingertips to her chin and brought them forward, almost like blowing a kiss—ASL for "thank you."

"Please come back soon, Lolly." Tessa mouthed the words along with her hand gestures. "We loved having you."

Beside him, Lolly bounced up and down. "And will you come to my dance recital on Christmas Eve? Please? I'm going to be Clara from *The Nutcracker*."

Julian grinned at her. "Of course we will."

"We'll all be there, Lolly. I promise." Emily patted the chair beside her. "Why don't you come sit beside me until it's time to go home?"

Emily shot Anders a wink as Lolly scooted away and settled beside her. She was clearly trying to give him as much alone time as possible with Chloe until they took Lolly home, and the message wasn't lost on his wife. She glanced at him with wide eyes, no doubt wanting him to play along and act as if they were real newlyweds who couldn't keep their hands off each other.

He moved to slide an arm around her and her earlier words rang in his head.

Last night was wonderful, but it should probably be a onetime thing.

Anders didn't want it to be a onetime thing. From the moment he'd opened his eyes, all he could think about was reaching for her beside him, burying his hands in her softly tangled hair and making love to her again. He still couldn't quite wrap his mind around the fact that he'd misread the situation so profoundly.

Or had he?

The second his hand brushed against her back, a shiver coursed through her, sending a jolt of pure electric arousal straight to his groin. Her gaze shot to his, and in that brief, unguarded moment, he could see all the things she refused to say. Last night had meant something. She still wanted him—she might even want him as badly as he wanted her. She just didn't want to admit it.

He kept his arm draped around her shoulders and casually toyed with a lock of her hair, biting back a smile as her cheeks grew pink and she reached for her mimosa and took a healthy gulp.

"Have you two thought about a honeymoon?" Emily asked.

Anders arched a brow at Chloe. *Oh, I've thought about it. I'm thinking about it right now, and so are you, my darling bride.*

"Um..." Chloe's flush turned as red as Santa's plush suit.

"Give them time, Mom. Christmas is in less than two weeks. I'm sure they want to get through the holidays first." Allegra pointed her fork at Chloe. "Besides, you're in charge of *Baby Nutcracker*, remember? You can't go anywhere until after Christmas Eve."

"I'm not." Chloe's gaze darted toward Anders. Then she blinked and looked away.

Neither of them was going anywhere until after Christmas Eve, because that was the end date of their agreement. Lolly's guardianship hearing was first thing in the morning. Afterward, all bets were off.

The date rested so heavily on Anders's shoulders that he hadn't thought beyond it in weeks. It was as if the entire calendar ended right then and there.

Except now, he could almost see past it. Not entirely. He still had no idea what the days beyond Christmas Eve would look like. He desperately hoped they included Lolly. She was the reason he'd ended up in this absurd situation to begin with, after all. Now that he was married, he could finally breathe again. He could allow himself to believe that it would all work out and Lolly could stay.

But he wasn't altogether sure why he was suddenly so acutely aware of the days, weeks and months to come. He only knew, sitting beside his complicated, beautiful wife at that joyous table in Bennington 8, surrounded by people who'd been lied to—kind people, good people—that the day before Christmas wasn't an end date.

It was a beginning.

Of what, he had no idea. He'd taken Chloe to bed, but their marriage was still a sham. Nothing had changed, and yet somehow everything had. Because despite the mess they'd made, and despite the fact that when Chloe let him take her hand and wind his fingers through hers, he knew it was just for show, the glittering diamond on her finger sparked something deep inside him. Something he hadn't felt in a very long time.

Hope. It was the hope of a fool—a man who'd abandoned his controlled, exacting existence and had been grasping at straws, making things up as he went along, making a mess of disastrous proportions.

But it was all he had, at least until Christmas.

"Your apartment is lovely." Chloe crossed her arms as she looked out over the snowy landscape of Central Park.

She could see ice-skaters spinning circles on the pond below and horse-drawn carriages making a wide loop around the green-and-white-striped tents of the Christmas market in Columbus Circle. She'd never been in a penthouse like this before—or anywhere else, for that matter—with such a spectacular view of the city. It was breathtaking, like standing in the center of a snow globe.

It was also ridiculous, considering she'd married a man and was now seeing his home for the very first time.

Their home. For the time being, anyway.

How on earth had she gotten herself into this predicament?

"Thank you." Anders followed her gaze to the scene

below, then turned his back on the window and raked a hand through his hair. He glanced around the massive master bedroom, looking at anything and everything, but not at her. "You can have the bed. I'll take the sofa."

"Oh." She swallowed. It was silly, wasn't it? They'd just made love the night before and now they weren't even going to sleep in the same bed. Surely that wasn't necessary. The bed was huge, a California king, big enough to spend an entire night side by side without ever touching one another.

Probably.

"You don't need to sleep on the couch." She shook her head, but it was too late.

Anders had already pulled a pillow and blankets from a sleek armoire and was busy arranging his makeshift bed.

Fine. If that was the way he wanted things, so be it. At least having him a chaste ten feet away from the bed would make sticking to the no-sex rule a realistic possibility.

And she was determined not to break that rule again. As wonderful as last night had been, it had also been thoroughly confusing. For a minute, she'd actually begun to believe that they were really and truly married. She'd liked that feeling far more than she should have. And the pang in her heart at the sight of Anders's pillow on the sofa told her she'd done the right thing.

They were playing house. That was all this was, and she couldn't keep forgetting how it would end. She needed to protect her heart at all costs.

As if to prove her point, Anders shook his head and said, “It’s for less than two weeks. I’ll be fine.”

“Right.” She nodded, and smiled so hard that her cheeks started to hurt.

Anders didn’t smile back. If anything, the furrow in his brow deepened as he strode into the expansive, spa-like bathroom and closed the door.

Chloe shimmied out of her dress and into her pair of black and carnation-pink polka-dot pajamas before he could emerge, and then pulled the covers up to her chin. The sheets were cold to the touch, and being in the enormous bed all by herself made her feel very suddenly, very acutely alone. She wished Prancer could curl up beside her. She’d broken every pet parenting rule known to man and let the puppy sleep with her after she’d brought her home, but now the little dog had taken up residence in Lolly’s frilly canopy bed.

Lolly had begged, and Chloe immediately caved. She didn’t want to think about what that might mean when it was time to pack up her things and take Prancer back home with her, so she didn’t. Instead, she aimed all her frustration at Anders as he exited the bathroom.

“Really?” She glared at his bare chest and the tight-fitting boxer briefs, slung so decadently low across his hips. “That’s all you’re wearing to bed?”

Her mouth dropped open, agog, before she could stop it, and for the first time since they’d left the Bennington and arrived at Anders’s penthouse, his lips curved into a grin. Not just a cocky half smirk, but a full-on knowing smile. It was beyond annoying and just mortifying enough for Chloe to snap back to her senses and force her mouth closed.

"Yes, really." He planted his hands on his hips, drawing her attention even more directly to his chiseled abs—if such a thing was possible—and then lower, to the V-shaped muscle that disappeared below the waistband of his boxers. "Would you prefer I wear something else?"

Yes. Specifically, something *more.*

"Um, no. It's none of my business." Damn it, did her voice have to come out so breathy? She cleared her throat and continued. "It's freezing outside, though."

"Ah, so you're worried I might catch a cold." His smiled widened, as if he knew good and well that she was suddenly quite warm.

Damn him.

"Exactly." She'd rather play along and pretend she was worried about his health than admit the simple truth that having him nearly naked in the same room was, ahem, *distracting.*

She understood why they needed to share a bedroom. The judge at the guardianship hearing might question Lolly, and how would it look if she said Chloe and Anders didn't sleep together? Besides, the master suite was certainly big enough for the two of them. Although it seemed to be shrinking by the second the longer Anders stood there wearing next to nothing.

"Maybe you're right. I should probably put on something warmer. Flannel, maybe?"

She nodded. Flannel was exactly what this situation called for.

"Too bad I don't have any." He narrowed his gaze at her. "In case you haven't noticed, I'm not exactly the flannel-pajama type of husband."

Chloe's cheeks blazed with heat. He was baiting her, and she probably deserved it after the abrupt way she'd handled things earlier this morning at the Bennington. She doubted he'd touch her again, even if she asked him to. And she definitely wouldn't. But as she let herself remember what it had felt like to touch all that warm, male skin that was on such flagrant display in front of her, she couldn't help the way her gaze lowered from his eyes to his mouth.

She licked her lips. "What type are you?"

Their eyes locked, and for a long, loaded moment, neither of them said a word. Neither of them had to. She knew precisely what sort of memories were running through his head, because the same ones were running through hers. She'd been doing her best to push them away all day, but it was impossible. She couldn't look at him anymore without wanting him. Sleeping with him had been the worst possible mistake she could make. Why hadn't she realized that before she'd practically begged him to make love to her?

Actually, she'd been aware of the danger all along. She'd known giving herself to him would lead to trouble, but she'd done it anyway. Because she just couldn't help it. The more time she spent with Anders, the more attractive he became. He wasn't the cold, distant puppy thief she'd originally thought he was. She wished he were. It would make not sleeping with him so much easier.

"I'm the pretend type," he said. The rawness in his voice almost killed her. "Right?"

She didn't trust herself to speak, so she nodded instead.

"Right," he said quietly, turning toward the sofa.

She wasn't sure what time she finally fell asleep. For hours she lay awake in that cold, lonely bed, listening to the rhythmic sound of Anders's breathing and wishing things could be different. Wishing that, for once, she'd really be chosen by someone...by Anders.

This was going to be the longest two weeks of her life.

Chapter Twelve

"How's married life?" Penelope sat across the conference table from Anders, leafing through the packet of merger and acquisition papers for a meeting that was due to start in less than fifteen minutes.

"It's fine," he said automatically, because how else was he supposed to respond?

Was he supposed to admit that he'd barely slept a wink in the week since he and Chloe had been married, because if he let his guard down for even a second he might give in to the impulse to toss the covers aside, crawl into bed with her and cover her exquisite body with his? Was he supposed to say that he woke up hard for her every day, but he hadn't laid a finger on her since their wedding night?

"The ceremony was beautiful." Penelope arched

a brow. "Not at all what I expected, but certainly lovely."

Anders looked up from the document in his hands. "What exactly did you expect?"

She shrugged. "I don't know, just something less..."

Less real? *Join the club.*

"...warm, I suppose. Celebratory." She angled her head and studied him. "You've been awfully scarce around here lately. I'm beginning to think you found an actual bride after I turned you down."

Anders's jaw clenched. He was hoping they could forget the whole marriage contract thing had ever happened, and proceed with business as usual. He had enough relationship problems at the moment without adding Penelope to the mix.

Oh, so now you and Chloe are in a relationship*?*

"It's the holidays," he said with a shrug.

He'd spent a little more time out of the office than he usually did this time of year, but not enough to be noticeable. Or so he'd thought.

But things were different now. He had Lolly to think about. Plus, living with Chloe Wilde was like having one of Santa's helpers under his roof. The woman seriously loved Christmas. The first day he'd left her alone in the penthouse, he'd come home from work to find a Christmas tree in his living room. Not an elegant, professionally decorated artificial tree like the ones he usually had delivered, but a real tree. A noble fir, covered with strings of popcorn and ornaments Chloe and Lolly had made out of construction paper, glue and glitter.

The tree was a disaster, as was his apartment. He'd never get rid of all the glitter; it was everywhere. But Lolly was besotted with the scraggly tree that refused to remain fully upright in its metal stand, no matter how many times Anders crawled beneath its branches and tightened the screws holding it in place.

Likewise, she'd practically glowed the next night when Anders walked in the door and found Prancer darting around the apartment in a Santa costume, complete with a tiny white beard strapped to her chin. Once again, it had been Chloe's doing. The following day, he'd found himself coming up with an excuse to leave the office an hour earlier than usual. He'd been unable to concentrate as he sat at his desk wondering what he'd stumble upon next. A snowman on the terrace? A Christmas cookie bake-off in the kitchen?

Wrong on both counts. When he walked into the penthouse, Lolly and Chloe had been decked out in ugly Christmas sweaters, wrapping a package with his name on it. He was now the proud owner of an ugly Christmas sweater of his very own. It matched the one they'd bought the dog.

"Since when do you take any time off at Christmas?" Penelope rolled her eyes.

"What time off? I've been here until five every night this week."

"My point exactly. You're never out the door before seven." She studied him for a moment and then shook her head. "Oh my gosh, it's true, isn't it? Your marriage to Chloe isn't fake at all. It's real."

A pain flared in Anders's temple. "It's not. Can

we get back to business, please? The client is going to be here any minute."

Penelope waved a dismissive hand. "No, he won't. Eric Johnson is never on time. He thinks it's a display of weakness. You've been working with him long enough to know that."

Indeed he had, but that still didn't mean he wanted to discuss his marriage, fake or otherwise, with the woman he used to occasionally share a bed with.

Not that he'd given much thought to his ex. She didn't even qualify as an ex, really. What they'd shared had been convenient, and now it was over. He couldn't imagine picking things up with Penelope again, even after his marriage ended.

If it ended.

He swallowed. Of course it would end. They'd made a deal, and so far, nothing had changed. "It's a contract marriage. Everything will go back to normal after the guardianship hearing and Christmas have passed."

"Sure it will." Penelope resumed flipping through the pages of the merger acquisition.

Anders knew better than to push. He'd wanted the discussion to end, and it had. But he couldn't let it go. Not like that.

He sat back in his chair and crossed his arms, as serious as if they were putting together a stock offering. "What's that supposed to mean?"

"It means you're fooling yourself if you think the two of you will walk away from this brief holiday union unscathed. Marriage means something, whether you want it to or not. I tried to warn you, remember?" She shook her head. "Besides, I was there. I saw the way you looked at her on your wedding day. I saw the giant rock on her finger. You're not faking it, Anders. If you think you are, you're in for a rude awakening."

He opened his mouth to protest and then promptly closed it. They sat in silence while her words sank in and took root.

"You're wrong," he finally said quietly. Chloe had drawn a line in the sand, and he wasn't about to cross it again. His entire life had been turned upside down. He certainly didn't need to invite any more chaos into it by trying to throw their arrangement out the window and asking her to marry him for real.

Besides, that was not what he wanted at all. Sure, he might like the throaty sound of her laughter and the silly, high voice she used when she talked to Prancer. He might spend long minutes at his desk thinking about the softness of her skin or remembering how the scent of her hair on their wedding night mirrored the blooms in her bridal bouquet. But that didn't mean he wanted to love, honor and cherish Chloe for the rest of his life. Did it?

Hell no, it didn't. He wasn't thinking straight, that was all. He was still grieving the loss of his brother, and everyone knew grief made people crazy. That was why the experts in such matters always urged grieving people not to make any major life decisions. Getting married—or, in his case, *staying* married—definitely qualified.

Penelope held up her hands. "I stand corrected,

then. After Christmas, you can stick to the terms of the contract the two of you signed and go your separate ways."

He looked away. He wasn't about to admit that he'd never drafted a contract. Penelope would have a field day psychoanalyzing that little tidbit.

"But I hope you don't, because I know one thing for a fact." She gave him a knowing smile. "You never once looked at me the way you look at Chloe."

"Penelope..."

She held up a hand to stop him. "If you're about to apologize, save your breath. I'm not jealous. I could have been Mrs. Anders Kent myself. I'm just saying you might want to consider the possibility that you've been given a precious gift, something that a lot of people spend a lifetime hoping for, before you throw it all away."

A precious gift, just like all the wrapped packages Chloe had been piling underneath their pitiful tree.

No. His teeth clenched, and he tightened his grip on his Mont Blanc. He and Chloe were pretending. She'd be gone and his life would be back to normal before that Christmas tree dropped its needles.

"You've got it all wrong," he said. Penelope's opinion on the matter didn't mean a thing to him, so he wasn't sure why he was trying to convince her she was wrong.

Maybe you're not. Maybe the person you're really trying to convince is yourself.

The unwelcome thought hit him like a ton of bricks

as Mrs. Summers appeared in the doorway to the conference room.

"Mr. Kent." She smiled at him, and then her head swiveled to Penelope. "Ms. Reed."

"Yes?" he said, grateful for the interruption. Short of the entire firm crumbling into ruin, he would have been thankful for just about anything to get his mind off of the woman who'd been sleeping in his bed, *by herself*, for the past seven nights.

"Your client is here. Shall I send him in?"

He nodded. "Yes, thank you."

Thank God.

Work was precisely what he needed at the moment. He could handle work. He was good at it, unlike everything else in his life.

But as the day wore on and he guided Eric Johnson through the terms of his pending acquisition, his mind kept wandering. And when the meeting wrapped up shortly before four o'clock, he put away his things and strode past the receptionist's desk without bothering to tell her where he was headed.

He'd had enough commentary on his personal life for one day.

Chloe glanced at the time on her phone as she stepped off the elevator in the lobby of Anders's posh building and hastened her steps.

Emily wasn't expecting her at the studio until six o'clock, which meant she'd be nearly an hour early, even navigating the subway during rush hour. But Lolly wasn't home, and Chloe had been doing her absolute level best not to spend any time with Anders alone in the penthouse.

It was a desperate plan, made all the more desperate by the fact that, thus far, hanging out with both Anders and Lolly hadn't lessened her attraction to her temporary husband at all. Even the ugly Christmas sweater had backfired. She'd never seen a man look so insanely hot in garish plaid with tiny little stockings hanging from his chest.

Watching him interact with Lolly was even worse. He was so patient with her. So kind. It killed Chloe to think he could end up losing her. The thought of Lolly being taken away from him was the only thing keeping her from packing her bags and pulling the plug on their excruciating arrangement. Every night she spent in Anders's bed without Anders was another exercise in self-torture. But she couldn't bring herself to walk away, not if it meant leaving him high and dry on the date of the guardianship hearing.

One week down, one to go.

She could do this. She could definitely hold out another seven days now that she'd begun overhauling the Wilde School of Dance. Anders had wired half the money he owed her into her account on the day following the wedding, and she'd wasted no time lining up all the necessary improvements. The new lobby furniture wouldn't be delivered until after the holidays, but she'd managed to schedule the floor installation for the upcoming weekend. Come Christmas Eve, *Baby Nutcracker* would be performed on a gorgeous new dance surface. If that didn't increase enrollment in the New Year, nothing would.

An extra hour or so at the studio wouldn't kill her, especially if it meant she could avoid the ridiculous breathless feeling she always got when Anders walked in the penthouse door at the end of the day and scooped Lolly into his arms. Even Prancer had gotten in on the honey-I'm-home action, running circles around Anders and nipping at his designer shoes while Chloe stood there like a third wheel.

If she was really being honest with herself—brutally, painfully honest—she didn't feel like a third wheel. When Anders would meet her gaze over the top of Lolly's little head, it took every ounce of her willpower not to join in on the affectionate display. They weren't a family and they never would be, but in those moments, they looked like one on the outside. And on the inside, they felt like one. No matter how very hard Chloe tried to deny it.

She had no idea what that domestic scene would feel like minus Lolly, and she was afraid to find out, hence her hasty exit from the penthouse a good half hour before Anders ever came home. But right after she waved goodbye to the doorman and bent her head against the afternoon snowfall, she plowed straight into the very man she'd been trying so desperately hard to avoid. Her husband.

"Whoa."

His voice was as deep and gravelly as ever, and the only thought running through her head as she collided face-first into his solid wall of a chest was that she needed to back away. Far, far away. Because he smelled so good, so manly, like warm cedar and pine, and his cashmere coat was so impossibly soft against her cheek that she was on the verge of purring like a kitten.

What on earth was wrong with her?

She must be in some kind of withdrawal. There'd been no physical contact between them whatsoever since the morning after they'd slept together. The last time he'd touched her had been over brunch at Bennington 8, and that generous dose of PDA had been for the benefit of her family. It had all been for show.

And whose fault is that?

Hers. Anders had done exactly as she'd asked and kept his hands to himself.

And it was driving her crazy.

"Sorry." She jerked backward before she made a complete idiot out of herself. She needed space. Loads of space—several feet, if possible.

But it was too late, because Anders's hands were already planted on her shoulders, steadying her, even as her legs went wobbly. She'd actually gone weak in the knees, like the world's biggest cliché.

He let out a little laugh. "Where's the fire?"

Everywhere. She nearly said it out loud, but stopped herself in the nick of time. The air was thick with a wintry mix of snow and frozen drizzle, and still she'd gone molten from his touch.

"Nowhere. I just..." She wiggled out of his grasp so she could form a coherent thought. "What are you doing home so early?"

His arms hung there for a second, as if they didn't know what to do now that his hands were no longer resting on her shoulders. Then he cleared his throat and shoved his hands in his pockets. "It's not that early."

"Yes, it is." She was keenly aware of what time Anders came home from work. Her self-preservation depended on it. So long as she knew when to expect him, she could put up her invisible shield, perfectly designed to keep him at arm's length.

Chloe wasn't good at surprises, particularly when those surprises included her charming pretend husband. Since their night together at the Bennington, it seemed like the biggest charade in her life wasn't their marriage at all, but instead the daily pretense that everything between them was still just platonic. When she was prepared, she could put on a decent act, in the same way that hours of rehearsal and time in front of the lit makeup mirror backstage used to prepare her for a performance. Everyone at Radio City knew what time the heavy red velvet curtain rose. Showtime was calculated down to the second. If the curtain had ever gone up a minute or two early, there would have been chaos.

And now the chaos was inside her heart, beating wildly at the sight of Anders on the busy snowy sidewalk, with a cozy Burberry scarf wrapped around his neck and his hair just windblown enough to remind her what he looked like when he climbed out of bed in the morning.

She swallowed. What *was* he doing home so early?

"Things were slow at the office." He was lying. Chloe had seen his calendar, and his phone chimed day in and day out with messages from his assistant, Mrs. Summers. Things were never slow at Anders's office.

He glanced up, toward the penthouse. "I thought I'd see what you and Lolly were up to this afternoon."

Lolly. Of course. He'd come home to spend time with his niece, which was sweet. Really, really sweet. Chloe wasn't sure why the shrinking feeling in her chest felt so much like disappointment.

"Lolly isn't here. She's still at the studio. Allegra let her stay for tap class and beginning ballet because she wasn't ready to go home after our recital rehearsal." The little girl was becoming more besotted by the day. It made Chloe even more determined to not only save the dance school, but help make it thrive again. "I think you might have a future dancer on your hands."

"Just like you." Something in his gaze softened, and it made the breath hitch in Chloe's throat. "That wouldn't be the worst thing in the world."

Their eyes locked, and for a dizzying second, everything around them faded away. The city streets, always humming with the blur of taxis and siren wails, faded into the background, until all she could see was the unexpected softness in his gaze and all she could hear was her pulse roaring like a wildfire in her ears.

Her family still didn't know she'd been fired. Only Anders knew the truth, and here he was, telling her he'd be happy if Lolly grew up to be just like her.

She shook her head. "I'm not a dancer anymore. Remember?"

"You'll always be a dancer," he said simply, and with enough conviction that she almost believed it.

She took a deep breath. "I should go. I need to get back to the studio."

"Isn't the nanny with Lolly? She can bring her home."

The nanny. Right. He still didn't know.

"I gave the nanny a week off. I hope it's okay. I just figured since it was Christmas she might want to spend some time with her own family, and I'm here now." *It's only temporary, remember?* As if she could forget. "But don't worry—she'll be back the day after Christmas."

He nodded as a cold understanding passed through his gaze. He'd need the nanny again once the expiration date on their makeshift family had passed. "I see. And of course it's okay."

"I should go." She couldn't keep standing there chatting about the nanny and Lolly's schedule, as if they were a real couple. A real family. "I need to get back to the studio."

"Aren't you finished teaching for the day?" he asked, before she could take a step.

"I am." She couldn't help but smile, despite her very real, very pressing urge to flee. *Baby Nutcracker* was one thing that seemed to be going right in her life. "Class was great today. You should have seen the kids working on the dance of the snowflakes choreography. It was adorable."

"I'm looking forward to seeing it Christmas Eve."

"Of course." Her smile faded, as it always did when someone mentioned Christmas Eve. It had always been her favorite day on the calendar, but not anymore. Not this year. "Anyway, I'm going back to do a little painting after hours."

"Painting?" He angled his head, and peering into his blue eyes was so like lifting her face to a crystal-clear sky that she had to look away.

She aimed her focus across the street, where a group of tourists was gathered around a Salvation Army volunteer ringing a bell and lip-synching to Mariah Carey Christmas songs. "I'm making a few improvements at the school. You know, so we can put our best foot forward at the recital."

"And you're painting the walls yourself?" He seemed puzzled, but then again, Chloe supposed billionaires typically didn't spend their off-hours doing manual labor.

"Yes." She lifted a brow. "It's really not that difficult. You should try it sometime."

He shrugged and his mouth curved in a half smile. "Okay."

And then, before she could wrap her mind around what he was doing, he moved past her toward the curb with his arm raised. A black town car materialized out of nowhere, because of course Anders Kent was the sort of man who got what he wanted, exactly when he wanted it.

It was beyond annoying, especially when he looked at Chloe as if the thing he wanted most of all was her.

One more week. That's all.

"What are you doing?" She made no move toward the curb, where he stood holding the door of the sleek black car open for her. And she tried her best not to look at the leather interior of the back seat or think about how much warmer and comfortable it would be than the subway.

"I'm going with you to help you paint. You said I should try it sometime." He leaned against the car and crossed his feet at the ankles, clearly prepared to wait things out while she tried to come up with an excuse to turn him down.

"But you're wearing a suit. You can't paint dressed like that."

"Watch me." He held out his hand, reaching for hers, and all she had to do was walk away, toward the subway station. Or make some kind of excuse to go back upstairs, and then she could leave in a little while, once he was busy with a work call or something.

She didn't do either of those things, though. Instead, she placed her hand in his and let him help her into the car, telling herself all the while that it would be fine. They'd be painting the walls, not slow dancing. Besides, no one fell into bed doing manual labor together.

But nestled beside her husband in the warm car, while twilight descended on the city and Manhattan shimmered in the golden glow of twinkle lights, looking as radiant as it could only at this time of year, she had to fight the urge to rest her head on his shoulder.

To press her thigh against his just to feel the solid warmth of his presence before she lost it. To climb into his lap and kiss the winter chill from his lips.

And then she began to realize that falling into bed shouldn't be her biggest worry.

After all, she was a dancer, and as every ballerina knew, there were far more dangerous ways to fall.

An hour later, when there was a brush in Anders's hand and paint splatters covering his oxford shirt and bespoke wool dress pants, he was willing to admit that he probably should have changed clothes before heading to the studio.

All the same, he had no regrets. If he'd paused long enough to go upstairs and change, he would've given Chloe the opportunity to leave without him. And he couldn't bear the thought of being stuck in the empty penthouse all evening.

He'd lived alone his entire adult life, so he should have felt perfectly content in an empty apartment. But he'd grown accustomed to the happy chatter that had filled the space for the past seven days. He liked the pitter-patter of Lolly's tiny feet as she chased Prancer around the Christmas tree. He liked listening to Chloe's voice—as silvery and lovely as tinsel. He liked falling asleep at night knowing that she was in the same room, even though the small amount of feet that separated them felt like miles.

She was *there.*

A week from now, she wouldn't be.

He wanted to hoard what time he had left with her

as if it were gold, and if that meant that one of his best suits suddenly looked like something straight out of the Museum of Modern Art, then so be it.

"You're surprisingly good at this." Chloe watched as he covered the last bare patch of wall with color in the main classroom.

They'd been alone for hours, sometimes painting in comfortable silence, sometimes talking about all the time Chloe had spent here as a child. He liked hearing new details about her life, filling in the blanks of her past and getting to know her better. He'd seen the tiny flare of panic in her eyes when Emily and Allegra had left for the evening, taking Lolly with them for another cozy Wilde sleepover.

He also knew what that look meant—his wife was trying her best not to be alone with him. But they'd needed this. He was tired of pretending their night together had been a mistake. It hadn't been a mistake at all.

It had been perfect.

And the way he kept catching her looking at him tonight when she thought he wasn't paying attention told him she thought so, too.

She glanced at him again, her gaze flitting from his hands to his mouth to his eyes before she flushed and looked away. "Seriously, is there anything you can't do? I would have never expected a legendary bachelor businessman to be handy with a paintbrush."

"I'm not a bachelor anymore, remember?" He arched

a brow at her and carefully placed his brush in the drip tray. "And there are plenty of things I can't do."

She rolled her eyes. "Like what?"

"Like dance. I'm a hopeless disaster on the dance floor."

Her mouth dropped open, giving him a tantalizing glimpse of her perfect, pink tongue. "I don't believe you."

He held up his hands. "Would I lie to a dancer about my having two left feet?"

"Be honest." Her gaze narrowed. "Is this outrageous falsehood just an attempt at getting me to slow dance with you?"

He reached behind her and gave her ponytail a playful tug, eliciting a wholly satisfying gasp. "There's only one way to find out, isn't there?"

"Well." He could see the wheels turning in her pretty little head. She had the same little furrow between her brows that she always got when he undressed for bed. Temptation. "I suppose I owe you a dance lesson, since you just spent your evening painting with me and ruined your suit."

"One dance, then we'll call it even. Deal?" He offered his hand for a shake.

She took it in her own, and the simple, innocent contact of her fingertips brushing against his was enough to make him hard. He didn't just want her. He *craved* her. He'd been craving her for a week straight.

"Deal." She smiled. "Do you think we'll ever have a normal, spontaneous interaction or will everything we do together be part of some kind of prenegotiated arrangement?"

He waited to answer until she slid an album out of its cardboard sleeve, situated it on the record player, and strains of something sultry and French filled the air.

"Well?" she asked, after she'd walked back toward him and stood close enough for him to see the tiny gold flecks in the depths of her beautiful brown eyes. "Do you?"

"I really don't care one way or another, so long as I get to touch you…" He slid a hand around her to the small of her back. "…here."

She bit back a smile.

"And here," he said, taking her hand in his so that they were in a traditional dance hold.

"Well played, husband," she murmured, as they swayed to the music.

"Thank you, wife," he whispered into her hair.

They stayed like that, hand in hand, thigh to thigh, reveling in the familiar heat of one another…waltzing… wanting…until long after the music ended and their only accompaniment was the sound of their hearts, beating as one.

"Just as I suspected," Chloe said, lips moving softly against his neck. "You lied. You're a fantastic dancer."

He let out a low aching laugh. "We have to stop, or we're going to have to renegotiate another one of our key terms."

She pulled away just enough to meet his gaze. "I thought you'd never ask."

Then she rose up on tiptoe and kissed him as if she had every intention of welcoming him into her bed again, which she did.

Every single night until Christmas Eve.

Chapter Thirteen

"All rise. The Family Court of the City of New York is now in session, the Honorable Judge Patricia Norton presiding." The bailiff stood in the corner of the room with his hands folded neatly in front of him as a robed woman entered the paneled room.

This is it, Anders thought as he rose to his feet. This was the moment that had been hanging over him since he'd learned about the special provisions in Grant's and Olivia's wills. Had it really been less than a month ago? It felt like years since he'd last seen his brother's face. So much had changed. He wondered what Grant would think if he could see him now, standing alongside Chloe.

Would he be proud?

Shocked?

Probably some combination of both, at least until he realized the marriage wasn't real. The fact that Anders had been desperate enough to hire a wife wouldn't have come as a shock to his brother at all. A disappointment, sure. But not a surprise. Everyone knew Anders Kent wasn't a family man.

Strangely enough, he felt like one now. Something about finally being face-to-face with the person who would decide whether or not he would be Lolly's father figure brought out a fiercely protective instinct that had him gripping the wooden railing separating the bench from the courtroom's front row, where he, Chloe and Lolly had been waiting with Anders's attorney. He glanced at them—at Lolly's dainty, innocent face and Chloe's exquisite, feminine features—and a familiar sense of panic seized his chest.

For weeks, the three of them had been living under the same roof. They'd eaten meals together, shared secrets and hung stockings from the mantel with their names spelled out in glitter. For six nights running, he and Chloe had spent their nights in the same bed, touching, kissing, loving. What had started out as a charade no longer felt like one. And as he looked at them now, he realized why the hollow feeling he'd felt right after Grant's accident was beginning to gnaw at him again…to consume him.

It was because some way, somehow, while they were pretending to be a family, they'd actually become one. Lolly and Chloe were his. No matter what happened here today, they would both be etched on his heart forever.

And now he might lose them both.

"You may be seated," Judge Norton said, peering down at a stack of papers on her desk after giving the people in her courtroom a cursory once-over.

Anders bit down hard, clenching his teeth. He clasped his hands in his lap to keep them from shaking.

Not now. Don't fall apart now.

He'd been handling things so well. Granted, he still couldn't bring himself to open the door to Grant's office and walk inside, but their argument was no longer the first thing his mind snagged on when he woke up in the morning or his final thought before he closed his eyes at night. He hadn't forgiven himself, because how could he? But he'd managed to push those feelings aside and get on with things. He was functioning again. He was in control, just like always.

Or so he'd thought.

"Our first order of business will be the matter of the guardianship of Lolly Kent." The judge looked up from her papers. "Is Mr. Anders Kent present?"

"Yes, Your Honor," Anders said, with a tremor in his voice that he'd never heard before—not even when he'd had to tell Lolly her parents were gone and they were never coming back.

Chloe reached for his hand and squeezed it tightly. He didn't dare look at her. To his horror, he realized that if he did, tears might well in his eyes. He hadn't shed a tear since his parents died. Even then, at seventeen, he'd cried only once—at the funeral, and never again.

"Hello, Mr. Kent." Judge Norton nodded in his

direction. "I assume you have an attorney here representing you, as well?"

Anders's attorney stood, introduced himself and asked to approach the bench. He passed Lolly's birth certificate to the judge, along with copies of Grant's and Olivia's wills and the crisp new marriage license signed at the bottom by Anders and Chloe.

It was all happening so fast. Too fast. The judge barely looked at the stack of documents before she motioned for Lolly to come forward. Lolly's little head swiveled toward Anders, her eyes wide.

"It's okay, sweetheart. She just wants to ask you a few questions." He gave his niece the most reassuring smile he could manage.

They'd known this was coming. The attorney had warned Anders and Chloe that the judge would want to talk to Lolly and ask her what living with Anders had been like. But he'd failed to tell Anders that his heart would feel like it was being ripped right out of his chest when he watched her walk toward the front of the courtroom.

"This will all be over soon," Chloe whispered. "It's going to be fine."

He dropped his gaze to his lap, where her hand still rested on top of his—covering, protecting. The diamond on her finger glittered, reflecting a kaleidoscope of light in all directions. And when he finally looked at her, it was with the knowledge that she'd done the same. She'd been a stranger who'd come into his life during its darkest moment, and she'd been more than just a convenient wife. She'd infused the darkness with goodness and light.

"Will it?" he asked. "Will it really be fine?"

Because suddenly, he didn't see how it could. The impending sense of doom in the pit of his gut wasn't about Lolly. Not entirely.

"Of course it will. Watch and see." She smiled.

I don't want to lose her. She turned away, toward the bench where the judge was speaking in whispered tones with Lolly. *I* can't *lose her.*

Neither of them had said a word about what might happen after today. As far as he knew, they'd part ways on the steps of city hall the minute all this was over. They'd had a deal, and they'd both done their part.

But deals could be renegotiated. He handled mergers and contracts on a daily basis. He excelled at it. He'd simply talk to her after the hearing and suggest an extension of their arrangement. They could postpone their separation, and maybe even date like two normal people.

It would all work out. It had to. Right now he just needed to think about it rationally, like a business deal, so he could get through the rest of the guardianship proceedings.

"Thank you, Lolly." Judge Norton leaned forward and handed the little girl a candy cane. "You may sit down now. I'll make the rest of this quick since it's Christmas Eve. I'm sure you're anxious to get home. We all are."

Lolly thanked the judge in a bubbly, animated voice,

prompting a titter of laughter through the courtroom. Even Anders managed a chuckle. Now that he had a plan, he could breathe again.

"All right, everything seems to be in order. It looks as though all the provisions of the guardianship have been met, and Lolly is clearly thriving under the care of Mr. Kent. I see no reason why custody can't be granted at this time." Judge Norton reached for her gavel. "I hereby appoint Anders Kent as the permanent guardian for Lolly Kent."

The gavel came down hard on the bench, marking an end to so many weeks of worry and speculation.

"Merry Christmas, Mr. and Mrs. Kent. You, too, Lolly." The judge winked. "You're a family now."

You're a family now.

The judge's words resonated in Chloe's mind with the utmost seriousness as she, Anders and Lolly made their way out of the courtroom.

As relieved as she felt that Anders had been granted permanent custody of Lolly, Chloe had never felt like more of an impostor. Of all the lies she'd told in recent weeks, her wedding to Anders had been the biggest. She'd known that going in, obviously. But it hadn't really sunk in until moments ago.

She'd been so worried about getting her heart broken that she hadn't thought long and hard enough about all the other things that could have gone wrong. What if they'd been found out? What if Anders had lost Lolly?

The devastating potential had hit her like a blow while they'd been sitting inside the courtroom. She'd held Anders's hand, and she'd done and said all the right things. But inside, she'd been terrified. Now she was almost too shaken to be relieved.

It's okay now. She concentrated on breathing in and out as Anders exchanged parting words with his lawyer. *It's all over.*

But the finality of the matter was little comfort. What, exactly, was over? Just the worry about Lolly's custody?

Or her relationship with Anders?

She swallowed and did her best to smile as Anders embraced them both in a group hug. Chloe's father used to do the same thing when she'd been a little girl. He would wrap his big arms around Emily, and then Chloe and her siblings would pile in. Her dad called it a *family* hug, and it had felt so much like this one that she couldn't quite breathe all of a sudden.

Are we a family?

Are we really?

She stepped out of the embrace and crossed her arms, steadying herself.

They should have talked about what would happen today. She had no idea whether she'd be sleeping beside Anders again tonight, whispering his name as he made love to her, or whether he expected her to pack up her things and leave.

She almost wished they'd stuck to their original agreement. At least then she would have known where she stood.

"Are you all right?" Anders studied Chloe as Lolly

busied herself unwrapping her candy cane. "You've gone pale."

She nodded, blinking rapidly. "I'm fine. I just..."

I just don't know where we go from here.

I just think I might be in love with you.

She shook her head, trying to force the thought right out of it. Falling in love had never been part of the bargain. Sex was one thing, but love was another matter entirely. She didn't want to be in love. She couldn't...not with someone who might not love her back.

Been there, done that. Never again.

"Sorry. I promise I'm really fine." She cleared her throat and nodded toward the courtroom. "That was just more intense than I expected."

He curved an arm around her waist and pulled her close. "But it's over now."

There was that word again: *over.*

She stiffened against him, and something that looked suspiciously like hurt flashed in his sapphire eyes.

Chloe's cell phone rang from the depths of her purse, and she bent to search for it so she wouldn't have to see that terrible look on his face. "I should probably get this. It might be my mom or Allegra calling about the recital tonight."

Anders nodded and crossed his arms, and for a quiet, confusing moment, he looked exactly as he had the first time she'd ever laid eyes on him—all hard lines and chiseled resistance. It made her heart beat hard in her chest, and when she finally located her phone, her hands shook as she dragged it out of her bag.

"Oh," she said, frowning down at the device's small screen.

"Is it about the recital?" Anders asked.

"No." Chloe swallowed. "It's the Rockettes."

The contact information for Susan Morgan, the dance troupe's general manager, flashed on her phone's display. Chloe hadn't spoken directly to Susan since the day she'd been removed from the performance schedule. Her reindeer shifts were supervised by someone much further down the chain of command.

"Answer it." Anders arched a brow. "It could be good news, right?"

It could.

Or it could be bad news, but either way, knowing would be better than uncertainty. *Nothing* in her life was certain at the moment, especially her relationship status. Facebook needed to invent a whole new description for this scenario.

She fixed her gaze with Anders's and pressed the button to accept the call. "Hello?"

"Hello, this is Susan Morgan from the Rockettes. Is this Chloe?"

"Yes, it is. Hi, Ms. Morgan." She gave Anders a slight smile. Susan sounded cheerful, not at all like a person who was about to fire somebody on Christmas Eve.

"Excellent. Listen, Chloe. I know this is last minute, but I also know you're anxious to start performing again. I've heard you've been working really hard on the promotional end of things, and I assure you that your time spent on flyer duty hasn't gone unnoticed."

"That's good to hear." Chloe began to pace in front of the low bench where Lolly sat swinging her legs to and fro.

This was it. She was getting her job back, and her life was finally going to return to normal. Chloe had been waiting for this moment for a long time—since Thanksgiving Day.

She wasn't sure why it didn't seem as exciting as she'd thought it would.

"One of the girls in the touring company just sprained her ankle, and we need a replacement. If you're able to leave for Branson tomorrow, the spot is yours." Susan's voice brimmed with enthusiasm, as if she was Santa Claus granting Chloe's biggest Christmas wish.

"Branson?" Chloe's feet stilled, and Anders's eyes locked with hers. "I don't understand."

The Rockettes had a smaller group of dancers that toured the country, performing in various venues, from coast to coast. The touring company traveled by bus, and they were on the road for up to nine months of the year. Chloe had never performed with the touring group, nor did she know any of its members.

"If you want to get back onstage, this is your chance. The bus leaves tomorrow afternoon," Susan said.

"But tomorrow is Christmas."

Now it was Anders's face that went pale.

"I'm emailing you the details. Think it over and let me know as soon as possible." Chloe could hear Susan's fingers tapping on her computer keyboard.

"But I'm going to be honest with you, Chloe. This is a onetime chance. It's this or nothing. Understood?"

"Yes," Chloe said. "I do."

I do.

Wedding words.

She ended the call and glanced up at the puzzled expression on her husband's face.

"Good news?" he asked, and there was an edge to his voice that rubbed her entirely the wrong way.

He didn't know the facts, and besides, she wasn't sure she even wanted to go on tour. Shouldn't they talk about what was happening between them?

Was there anything happening between them, or had she simply been fooling herself all this time?

"Yes," she said woodenly. "They want me to join the touring company."

"I see." He cleared his throat. "Congratulations."

Seriously? That was all he had to say? *Congratulations?*

She still hadn't said she was actually going anywhere. And she didn't know what she expected him to say, but she definitely thought it would be something more than a single word.

Her chest grew tight, and a flare of panic hit her somewhere behind her breastbone.

Actually, a single word would have been fine. She just thought it would be a different one. The word she most wanted to hear wasn't *congratulations*; it was *stay.*

Oh God, he wasn't going to say it, was he? Their

deal was over, and he was perfectly fine with her turning around and walking away.

"The tour leaves tomorrow." What was she doing? She was acting as though she wanted to be on a bus to Branson tomorrow when that was not what she wanted at all.

She bit her lip and blinked up at him.

Please ask me. Please just say it.

Stay.

"I heard." He took a deep breath, and for a moment he looked at her in a way that reminded her so much of the way he had on their wedding day that her panic ebbed. Maybe she really did love him, and maybe—just maybe—he loved her, too.

But then his gaze shifted until he was no longer looking her in the eyes, but instead at a blank space slightly over her head. "A clean break is probably for the best."

He didn't mean it.

He couldn't.

She waited for a good three seconds, giving him as much of a chance as she could for him to take it back, to somehow make those terrible words go away.

But he didn't. He let them settle into her bones, into her soul, until the only thing she could do was turn around and walk away, with her heart breaking cleanly in two.

"But I don't understand." Emily Wilde's coffee sat untouched on the table in the cozy kitchen of the brownstone as she stared blankly at Chloe.

Breaking the news to her mom about the Rockettes tour wasn't going nearly as well as Chloe had expected, and she hadn't even gotten to the part about her marriage being a big fat fake. She'd hoped the pair of gingerbread lattes she'd picked up en route from the courthouse would soften the blow, but clearly it was going to take more than a Christmas-flavored beverage to worm her way out of the mess she'd created.

"Why would you leave to go on tour? It doesn't make any sense." Emily picked up the coffee and put it back down without taking a sip. Not a good sign.

Chloe took a deep breath. "Because if I don't go, I won't be a Rockette anymore."

It was time to tell the truth…about everything. "I lied about why I haven't been performing the past few weeks. I wasn't injured. I was fired."

She winced, waiting for the dressing-down that was surely coming. She definitely deserved it.

But instead of rebuking her, Emily just shook her head and smiled. "I wondered when you were going to get around to telling me the truth."

Chloe blinked. "You mean you knew?"

"Yes, dear. Of course I knew. I've been a ballet teacher long enough to know when a dancer is too hurt to perform and when she's faking it." She lifted a brow. "I'm also your mother, so I know when you're going through something. I didn't want to push. I figured you'd tell me when the time was right."

Her mother had known the entire time. Chloe wasn't sure whether that made her feel better or worse. Then again, she was about as low as she could possibly get at the moment. There was no *worse*. This was it. This was heartbreak.

She took a shuddering inhalation and blinked hard against the tears that she'd been holding back all afternoon. If she cried now, she'd never stop. All she had to do was get through the rest of the day and the recital later tonight. Once she was on a bus headed away from Manhattan, she could cry all she wanted.

"I guess now's the time." She gave her mom a watery smile. "I didn't want to tell you. I was ashamed because I'd put my career first for so long, and when it all came crashing down, I realized how much I'd missed my family. I wanted to make it up to you..."

"Oh honey. Is that what working at the school and the new floors and the rest of the improvements have been about?"

Chloe nodded. "Yes."

But that wasn't quite the truth, was it? Not all of it, anyway. And she didn't want to lie anymore. It was too exhausting. Lies had led her to where she was right now, and she'd never felt more lost. "It started out that way, but spending so much time there made me remember how much I love it. I don't want to see the school close, Mom. It can't."

Emily's lips curved into a bittersweet smile. "The school won't be there forever, but that's okay. If and when it closes, I'll be okay. So will you. In the end, it's just a building. The heart of the studio is our family, and family is forever. You don't need to ask my forgiveness or make up for anything. I love you unconditionally, sweetheart. I'm just glad you've finally come home, no matter what brought you back."

And now she was leaving again.

Chloe stared down at her coffee. She couldn't bring herself to meet her mother's gaze anymore. She knew what going on tour would look like. It would seem like she was running out on Anders and Lolly, like she was making her same old mistakes. Which was precisely why she didn't want to go.

She had to, though. Her pretend marriage had turned into a very real disaster. Anders had point-blank told her she should leave.

Perfect timing...a clean break.

The words kept spinning in her mind, over and over again. She couldn't make them stop.

"Stay," Emily whispered. Then she said it again, louder this time. "Stay, Chloe. Don't go on tour."

They were the words she'd longed to hear, the only words that mattered. But they were coming from the wrong person. "Mom, I can't..."

"I'm not asking you to stay for me or for the school. Stay for Anders and Lolly. They need you, but more than that, you need them."

Truer words had never been spoken.

She closed her eyes, and the judge's words came back to her.

Merry Christmas, Mr. and Mrs. Anders. You're a family now.

But they weren't. And she couldn't need Lolly and Anders. She had no right.

"There's something else." She pushed her coffee

cup away. The gingerbread scent was making her sick. It reminded her too much of reading Christmas stories to Lolly, decorating the tree in Anders's penthouse and the way she'd looked out his bedroom window and watched the skaters spinning round and round on the frozen pond below while he'd wrapped his arms around from behind and pressed tender kisses to her shoulder.

"I suspected as much," Emily said calmly. Too calmly, as if she knew exactly what Chloe was about to say.

Was her mother some kind of mind reader? Or was Chloe just *that* transparent?

The latter, probably. She felt as delicate as tissue paper right now. "The only reason Anders and I got married was so he could be appointed as Lolly's guardian. The hearing was earlier today."

There. She'd said it. She'd confessed all.

She'd been holding so much inside that she should have felt unburdened, but she didn't. It still felt as if there was a ten-pound weight attached to her heart.

"And?" Emily prompted.

Chloe swallowed. "He won. It's over."

"Are you sure those two things go hand in hand?" her mother asked quietly.

"Yes." She was tired of fooling herself. She couldn't do it anymore. Since the night Anders had helped her paint the studio, she'd let herself pretend their marriage bargain was in the past. Technically, there'd never been a formal contract. Maybe on some level,

Anders hadn't wanted one. Maybe she'd been different. Special.

Now she knew the truth. She wasn't. She could have been anyone.

"I'm not going to pretend that I didn't have doubts about you and Anders. It all came about very suddenly, but I supported you—as did the rest of your family—because you assured us it was what you wanted. Biting my tongue was hard, but not for long." Emily reached forward and cupped Chloe's cheek, forcing her to meet her gaze. "Look at me, sweetheart. Listen to what I'm saying. That man loves you. Maybe he can't articulate it, or maybe he hasn't realized it yet, but he does. It's been written all over his face since the morning after your wedding. He's been through a lot. He lost his brother, and from what you've said, he nearly lost Lolly. If you love him, too, you owe it to him to give him more time."

"He could have asked me to stay, but he didn't." Chloe choked on a sob. "It's too late."

"Oh honey, it's never too late. Not while you're still wearing his ring."

Chapter Fourteen

Chloe toyed with the diamond on her finger as the elevator carried her to the top floor of Anders's office building.

How could she have forgotten to return the ring?

She hadn't even realized she'd still been wearing it until her mother pointed it out. It had become part of her in the same way that a dancer's choreography became rote after enough repetition. Muscle memory, they called it. A body remembered what it was supposed to do—feet moved in time to music without the dancer having to give it conscious thought. Most people thought that memories lived only in the mind, but they were wrong.

And now the ring felt as if it belonged on her finger. The day Anders had given it to her, it felt so foreign, so strange. She couldn't stop looking at it, even though she knew it didn't mean anything. It was just a symbol, part of the charade.

Somewhere along the way, she'd forgotten that significant fact. It had become more than a ring. More than a diamond. It was a sparkling part of her heart, a memory belonging to the body's hardest-working muscle of all.

She slipped it off and tucked it into her coat pocket as the elevator slowed to a stop. Keeping it was out of the question. It had to be worth a fortune. But she definitely didn't want to return it to him at the recital later. She was planning on staying as far away from him as she possibly could. It was her only hope of getting through the night and doing her job without breaking down.

Nor did she want to go to the penthouse. If a clean break was what he wanted, she'd give him one. He was supposed to be out of the office all day, so she'd simply put it in an envelope and leave it in his desk drawer. She'd send him a text, so it wouldn't come as a surprise. It was the polite thing to do.

She shook her head. Good grief, their parting was all so civilized and businesslike, the complete opposite of a normal breakup. It was ending in the same way it had begun. Maybe that was fitting.

Or maybe you're still fooling yourself.

The elevator doors slid open, and there was nothing businesslike about the way her heart pounded when she pushed through the paneled entry of Anders's investment banking firm, or the way the diamond felt like it was burning a hole in her pocket—all light and heat, out of sight but not out of mind.

"Mrs. Kent." Anders's assistant, Mrs. Summers, knitted her brow as Chloe approached. "I'm afraid Mr. Kent isn't in right now. He took the afternoon off."

"Yes, I know." Her gaze darted toward the closed door to Anders's office. "I just need to drop something off. Is it okay if I go inside?"

"Of course. We're closing in just a few minutes, though, so everyone can run last-minute Christmas errands."

"It won't take long. Thanks so much." She wished Mrs. Summers a merry Christmas and then stepped inside the office, clicking the door shut behind her.

Chloe flipped the lights on and then paused, feeling like an intruder. The space was so quintessentially Anders, with the same sleek, classic decor as the penthouse. It even smelled like him, warm and woodsy.

She hadn't set foot in this building since the day she'd turned up in her reindeer costume to insist that Lolly keep the puppy, and instead had ended up engaged to be married. Something about the space seemed different, but she couldn't put her finger on it.

It didn't matter, though, did it? She just needed to leave the ring somewhere safe and get to the Wilde School of Dance so she could prepare for the recital. She had plenty to keep her busy until the touring company left town. If she just kept moving, maybe she'd get through the next twenty hours in one piece.

It wasn't until she crossed the room that she realized what was different about the office. A collection of shiny new picture frames decorated the bookshelves to the right of the desk. Her breath caught in her throat when she saw that each and every one of the photographs were of either her or Lolly. But then she turned her back on the frames and reminded herself that they were only props, just like her. All for show.

She moved behind Anders's desk, searching for an envelope. There weren't any—not anywhere on the desk and not in any of the neatly organized trays on the credenza. She should probably ask Mrs. Summers for one, but that might lead to questions that Chloe was in no way prepared to answer.

She was going to have to open one of the drawers and pray that no one walked through the door and thought she was snooping.

Just do it and get it over with.

Chloe slid open Anders's top center drawer as quickly as possible, but as soon as she saw what was inside, she froze.

It was a file folder labeled *Premarital Agreement*, and the sight of it caught her so completely off guard that she couldn't seem to move. Or breathe. Or even blink.

Was this the contract that Anders kept talking about in the beginning, but that never seemed to materialize? It had to be, right?

There was only one way to find out. And even though looking at it would be painful, maybe she needed to see it. Maybe it would remind her what she'd signed up for in the first place. Not a real relationship, and definitely not love.

Love.

Was she in love with Anders? She couldn't be, could she? People didn't fall in love in a matter of weeks. She was just suffering from an intense case of Christmas infatuation.

She flipped open the file folder, fully prepared for the words on the contract to reinforce her theory. If there was one way to convince herself she wasn't in love, seeing the details of their marriage spelled out in black and white would surely do the trick.

But the name at the top of the contract wasn't hers; it was Penelope's. The only contract in the folder was the very same one she'd spotted on Anders's desk weeks ago. She flipped through the entire stack of papers just to be sure, but her name wasn't on any of them. Only Penelope Reed's.

Chloe's name wasn't the only notable omission, either. None of the numbered pages included a single mention of an engagement ring.

But that didn't make sense. She'd specifically asked Anders if the sparkling diamond was part of the contract and he'd said yes. It was all part of the package—the package he'd first offered to Penelope.

Unless it wasn't.

For the first time since their tense exchange in the courthouse hallway, Chloe's heart felt as if it were expanding instead of shrinking into nothingness. Could it be true? Could the ring have been meant for her all along?

If so, maybe she'd never been just an interchangeable, convenient bride. Maybe what she and Anders had really meant something. Maybe it had all along.

Maybe it really *was* love.

She pressed a hand to her breastbone to try to calm the frantic beating of her heart. She wanted to believe Anders loved her. She wanted to believe she'd been different from the very beginning. She hadn't realized how very much she wanted to believe until right that second.

She squeezed her eyes closed tight and let herself imagine, just for a moment, that everything had been real. And a feeling so pure, so sweet wrapped itself around her heart that it was like Christmas Past, Christmas Present and Christmas Future all rolled into one. Timeless.

When her eyes fluttered open, the first thing her gaze landed on was a picture frame at the head of Anders's desk. Inside was a photograph of Chloe on their wedding day, and it wasn't facing outward like all the other newly framed pictures in the office. The photo faced Anders's chair, where only he could see it.

Her eyes swam with tears.

What had she done?

Her mother was right. She'd been so ready to believe Anders didn't love her that she'd acted as if she really wanted to go on tour, when all the while he'd been sitting at this desk every day looking at her picture. And now it was too late—too late to tell him she wanted more, too late to stay.

Or was it? Emily's words from earlier echoed in

her consciousness, as sharp and clear as if her mother was whispering them in her ear. *Oh honey, it's never too late. Not while you're still wearing his ring.*

Chloe picked up the diamond, and with tears streaming down her face, she gingerly slid it onto her finger.

Back where it belonged.

Anders moved in a daze after he left city hall.

He remembered holding Lolly's tiny hand in his, but he couldn't quite recall walking down the building's wide marble steps or sliding into the town car that waited for them at the curb. It was as if one minute he'd been standing in that awful, institutional hallway watching Chloe walk away, and the next, he was sitting inside the car, staring blankly at his driver's face in the rearview mirror, unable to answer the question that had been posed to him.

"Sir," the driver repeated, more slowly this time. "Shall we wait for Mrs. Kent?"

Anders blinked. Hard. "Ah, no. She won't be joining us."

The driver's gaze flitted briefly to the columned building, and his brow furrowed. Mercifully, he didn't press for an explanation. "Yes, sir."

Then the car was winding its way through the holiday traffic, and once again Anders felt as if he were in a dream—a garish nightmare in which everything around him was too loud and too bright. The tree in Rockefeller Center loomed over the block, dark and terrible, and the animated store windows on Fifth Avenue seemed to be moving in double time. Snow flurries whirled dizzily past the car window, making him sick to his stomach, so he closed his eyes and leaned against the headrest.

Anders loved Manhattan. He loved that he could walk down the street and hear multiple languages spoken all at the same time. He loved the way the subway was like a spool of Christmas ribbon, tying all the different parts of the city together, making it feel like he could be anywhere in a matter of minutes. He loved the way the lights of the surrounding skyscrapers made the East River shimmer at nighttime, like liquid gold.

Most of all, though, he loved the way the sidewalks and the streets pulsed with life at all hours of the day and night. All the hustle and bustle, all the noise—they made it easier to forget that sometimes his chest felt hollow and empty. Even the loneliest person in the world could feel a little less isolated in Manhattan.

But now the city he loved so much was betraying him. His life had come to a screeching halt, and everywhere he looked, people kept moving. Throngs of last-minute shoppers filled the streets, and the decorations that transformed the gray, urban grit into an enchanted wonderland—the giant stack of oversize red ornaments on Sixth Avenue and the neat rows of trumpeting angels that towered over Rockefeller Center—seemed more surreal than beautiful.

What the hell had just happened?

Lolly was safe. She was *his*. The judge had called the three of them a family, and immediately afterward, he'd somehow let Chloe walk away.

No, that wasn't quite right. He'd pushed her away.

A clean break is probably best.

He'd actually said those words, as if a clean break from Chloe was what he wanted, when it wasn't at all. He didn't want any kind of a break.

He tried to take a deep breath, but his throat closed up.

You did the right thing.

He'd done it for her. Chloe deserved better than what he'd offered her, better than a fake marriage to a man who'd made a mess of every personal relationship he'd ever had. She deserved the world.

He knew she wanted to dance again. She'd told him so herself at Soho House. If performing again hadn't meant so much to her, she wouldn't have kept turning up in Times Square in that crazy, blinking reindeer suit.

A smile came to his lips at the memory of the day they'd first met, at the animal shelter. He would never look at a reindeer the same way again. Or Christmas, for that matter.

Lolly tugged at the sleeve of his coat and he turned to face her. He needed to keep it together. But, damn it, how was he going to explain Chloe's sudden absence from the penthouse? On Christmas, no less. "Hey, sweetie."

"Your phone is ringing," Lolly said. "Don't you hear it?"

He hadn't heard it, probably because it was just part of the sensory overload that was bombarding him at the moment. So much noise, so many feelings...all pressing in around him.

"Thanks. I'll get it." He ruffled her hair and managed a smile. She grinned back up at him and then went back to sucking on her candy cane and looking out the window at the snowfall.

Anders pulled his ringing cell phone from his pocket, and for a brief moment of pure optimism, he thought perhaps it was Chloe. But it was the office, of course—at two in the afternoon on Christmas Eve.

Mrs. Summers's familiar contact information flashed on the display, and as if by rote, his thumb hovered over the accept-call button, but he stopped just shy of pressing it.

The old Anders would have answered the call in a heartbeat, but he didn't want to be that person anymore. He was Lolly's father figure now, the only family she had. He wanted to be better. He *needed* to be better. Whatever was happening at the firm could wait.

So he did something he'd never done before in his entire professional career. He let a call from his assistant roll to voice mail. And he had no qualms about it, until the phone started ringing again almost immediately afterward. Mrs. Summers never bombarded him with repeat calls. Then again, he usually picked up the first time.

Something was wrong. He could feel it. He wasn't sure what it could possibly be on Christmas Eve, but it had to be important.

He glanced at Lolly again, but her gaze was still

glued on the scene out the window, so he finally took the call. "Hello?"

"I'm sorry to bother you, Mr. Kent. I know it's Christmas Eve, and the office is about to close." Mrs. Summers's voice lowered to a murmur. "But Mrs. Kent is here, and she seems rather…sad…so I thought I should call."

Anders's heart hammered hard in his chest. "Chloe is there?"

"Yes. She's in your office. I hope it's okay that I let her go inside."

"It's fine." Chloe didn't want to see him. That much was obvious, since she knew he wouldn't be at the office. "I'm glad you called."

It's clearly over. Let it go.

"I was just on my way out, but I can stay if you like." She cleared her throat. "You know, in case you'd like me to keep her company and give you time to get here."

Subtlety had never been his assistant's strong suit. She'd obviously picked up on the fact that there was trouble in paradise.

Mrs. Summers knew the marriage was only temporary. So did Penelope. Why was he the only one who seemed to remember that significant detail?

Chloe remembers.

He ground his teeth. "Thank you, but that won't be necessary. You have a merry Christmas."

As soon as he ended the call, the driver met his gaze in the rearview mirror. "Mr. Kent, has there been a change in plans or are we still headed to the penthouse?"

"No, I..." Anders looked up and realized the car was sitting in traffic, gridlocked in the familiar landscape of the West Village. As usual, a crowd was lined up at Magnolia Bakery, just to his right. Right around the corner was the Wilde School of Dance.

Allegra would be there. So would Emily. If he stopped there now, they might be willing to watch Lolly for him if he wanted to get to the office and see Chloe...in private...for a proper goodbye. She deserved that much, didn't she?

By now, though, her family probably knew the truth. They'd probably despise him on sight.

Was he really that desperate?

A final goodbye. One last kiss.

Yes...yes, he was. "Actually, there's been a change of plans."

Chapter Fifteen

By the time Anders dropped off Lolly and made his way to the financial district in the Christmas Eve traffic, he was too late.

Allegra had greeted Lolly with open arms and treated him in the same easy, lovable manner she always did. Emily had been quiet and there'd been a bittersweet, knowing smile on her lips when he'd told her he needed to find Chloe so they could talk. She knew. He was certain of it. But she'd been nice enough not to mention that he hadn't exactly been the husband her daughter deserved, and said simply, "Go find Chloe. Lolly can stay here, and we'll see you later tonight at the recital."

There'd been such hope in his heart on the way, but now here he was, and his office was empty, as quiet as a tomb. There was no sign Chloe had even been there. If he hadn't gotten the call from Mrs. Summers, he would have never known.

He ran into the hallway, darting from room to room, searching for her—searching for some kind of hint as to why she'd shown up. It didn't make sense. Nor did his frantic hunt through the office, but he didn't know what else to do. He just knew he needed to keep moving, because if he dared stand still, the reality of her absence would be too much. Too real.

He stopped short of the door at the end of the hall—the room he'd been avoiding for weeks. His brow broke into a cold sweat and his hands clenched and unclenched at his sides, as if he was preparing for a fight.

But he was tired of fighting. So very, very tired. He'd been fighting for weeks—fighting his grief, fighting his feelings for Chloe, fighting anything and everything trying to make its way into his cold, dead heart.

He stared at the closed door, letting his gaze linger on the familiar name embossed on the wood paneling.

Grant Kent.

He reached a shaky hand toward the doorknob.

Now's not the time. Walk away.

When was the time, though? Was he going to avoid entering this room for the rest of his life? Was he just going to keep walking away every time he began to come face-to-face with what he'd lost…?

Just like he was doing now.

Just like what you did with Chloe.

His hand clamped down on the knob and turned.

Then he pushed the door open as he'd done a thousand times before, only this time it wasn't to crunch some numbers or argue over an IPO or a contract or a million other things that Anders had always thought were so important but never really mattered.

This time, he was here to say goodbye.

He walked inside, marveling at how normal everything seemed. Papers were still strewn all over Grant's desk, and if his laptop hadn't been closed, it would have looked as if he'd just stepped out for a minute and would be right back. It smelled the same, too, like the aftershave Grant used after his lunchtime gym sessions, with just a hint of the Cuban cigars he brought out whenever one of them pulled off a significant business deal. Light streamed in the windows through a lacy veil of frost and snow, making it seem as if the office had been frozen in time.

Anders knew better.

Time kept spinning forward. People moved on.

Only if you let them.

The words came to him, as clear and distinct as if Grant had spoken them out loud.

"What are you trying to tell me, brother?" Anders whispered.

Great. He was talking to ghosts now.

Except there were no ghosts here. Anders knew that. If Grant's spirit lingered anywhere, it wouldn't be in this room. He'd be somewhere else, someplace more meaningful. Someplace where he could see his daughter or the spot where he'd first kissed Olivia or even Yankee Stadium for an afternoon of beer and baseball. His brother worked to live, not the other way around. How many times had he tried to explain that to Anders?

He still hadn't learned. Today was Christmas Eve, and look where he was standing. What was he doing?

Searching for her.

Searching for a life like the one his brother had lived. Searching for love.

He *loved* Chloe.

How could he have thought otherwise, even for a second?

If she wanted to go on tour, that was fine. He'd support her in whatever she chose to do, but she needed to know that when she came home, he'd be right there waiting for her. So would Lolly. And even Prancer, too.

Because they were a family.

He'd made a vow, and he intended to keep it—not because of some stupid agreement or because he needed a wife, but because he wanted one. He wanted *her*, and it was time he let her know. He'd gotten here too late and she wasn't here, but he knew where to find her.

Anders took one last look around, remembering all the time he'd spent in this office. Times when he and Grant had laughed, times when they'd argued. Somehow he'd forgotten that the former far outweighed the latter. Echoes of that laughter rolled over him now, and he realized that no matter what Grant's intentions had been when he'd signed his will, the marriage provision on Lolly's guardianship had ended up being a gift—a fateful, final Christmas present from one brother to another, the gift Anders needed most of all.

Thank you, brother.

"Where's Uncle Anders?" Lolly peered through the classroom window as Chloe wound a pink satin ribbon around the little girl's high ponytail.

Baby Nutcracker was set to start in just ten minutes. Lolly was all dressed up in her Clara costume—a long ruffled nightgown with a fluffy petticoat that swished around her slender legs when she twirled. Her face had lit up like a Christmas tree when she'd first put it on, and ever since she'd taken that initial glimpse of herself in the mirrored walls of the studio, she'd been asking for Anders.

"He'll be here. I know he will. He wouldn't miss this for the world," Chloe whispered and gave the little girl a kiss on the cheek. "It's probably good that he hasn't seen you yet. Won't he be surprised when you chassé onto the stage?"

Lolly nodded and giggled, appeased for the time being, and Chloe guided her to the spot off to the side of the classroom where the other kids were seated and waiting for the performance to start. They had six mice, six snowflakes, three sugarplums and a few fairies and snow queens. But as Lolly pointed out with pride, only one Clara. She was the star of the show.

And her uncle was nowhere in sight.

"Mom," Chloe whispered, pulling Emily behind the Christmas tree in the lobby—the closest thing to privacy they could get, since the school was filled with wall-to-wall parents, grandparents and siblings, all waiting to watch the adorable holiday spectacle. "Anders still isn't here. What *exactly* did he say when he dropped Lolly off earlier?"

"He said you were at his office and he needed to talk to you about something." Emily took a deep breath. "Something important."

They'd missed one another, which wasn't surprising, considering the streets were filled with last-minute shoppers and people on their way to Christmas Eve services at church or other holiday celebrations...like the one she was in charge of, starring his niece. Which was supposed to start in less than five minutes.

She tried her hardest not to think about what he'd wanted to say to her, but possibilities kept pirouetting through her head, each one worse than the next.

He'd had goodbyes in his eyes back at city hall, and he probably wanted to get the ring back. Or the key to his penthouse. Things he couldn't have said in front of Lolly.

Of course Mrs. Summers had called and told him Chloe was there. She didn't know why she hadn't anticipated it, other than she hadn't been thinking clearly. She'd been moving on autopilot, doing her best to survive until she went on tour the following day.

There would be no tour now. No more sequined reindeer costumes, no more passing out flyers in Times Square. Not for Chloe. She'd already called and officially resigned from the Rockettes roster. She wanted to teach full-time at the Wilde School of Dance. She wanted to stay right where she was, and if Anders still wanted a clean break, she'd give him one. She'd move into the Wilde family brownstone if she had to, but she wasn't leaving New York. She was home to stay.

"Lolly will be crushed if he doesn't get here in time," she said, just as the overhead lights dimmed. She waved her arms at Allegra, standing on the other side of the room, trying to signal for her to slow down. To wait just a few more minutes. But her sister-in-law was already placing the needle of the record player on the smooth, rotating surface of the Tchaikovsky album.

The opening bars of the beloved *Nutcracker* score filled the air, and Chloe couldn't wait any longer. It was time for her to lead the children onto the center of the new Marley floor for the beginning party scene.

"Look, dear." Her mother gave her arm a squeeze. "He's here."

Her heart gave a not-so-little pang, and beyond the fragrant boughs of the evergreen tree, she saw Anders push through the front door of the studio and rush into the classroom.

He stood in the very back, against the wall, where, as usual, his presence seemed to fill up the space and steal the breath from Chloe's lungs.

She stared at him for a beat, frozen, until Emily cleared her throat. "Are the children going to hit their cue, or are we going to have to start the music over again from the beginning?"

Right. There was a recital happening, and she was the person in charge of it.

"I'm on it!" Chloe slipped as discreetly as possible to where the kids sat, waiting to go on.

Chloe's mom had always believed in holding recitals for the very young children here in the school rather than in a stuffy auditorium. Her theory was that the familiar, intimate setting made it less scary for the kids, which definitely seemed to be the case. Three-year-olds, four-year-olds and five-year-olds needed encouragement, not an intimidating introduction to performing that could lead to debilitating stage fright.

She crouched down and gave them a last-minute pep talk as the prelude started to wind down. "Remember, guys, this is just like class. Only this time you're all dressed up, and tonight is Christmas Eve."

Miraculously, they all glided to the center of the floor, hand in hand, just as Chloe had taught them. She considered it a minor victory that none of the little ones cried, although one of the mice stood, holding the tail of her costume for a full minute or two, instead of doing the simple somersault combination they'd been practicing every day for a week. But about a third of the way into the program, she finally started moving her feet.

Chloe stood off to the side, marking the choreography with subtle movements so her students could follow along in case they got confused. Her position so close to the mirror allowed her to steal a glance every so often at Anders, still positioned at the back of the room.

His attention was trained on Lolly, who floated across the floor with a wide smile and a wave for her uncle. He waved back at her, and then, so quick that Chloe almost thought she'd imagined it, his gaze locked with hers in the mirror. He winked.

Then, in a flash, he was watching the performance again, and she was left to wonder if it had really happened. Had her temporary husband just shot her a flirty little wink just hours after they'd agreed to a clean break? If so, this might not be such a blue Christmas, after all. It could possibly be the best she'd ever had.

It took every ounce of concentration she could muster to keep miming the footwork for the kids, but the half-hour program passed quickly, punctuated by hearty applause and several bursts of laughter from the parents. In the end, even the children were surprised when the wind machine Chloe had secretly rented from a Broadway theater company blew tiny bits of fake snow all over the makeshift stage.

The audience rose to its feet as the classroom was transformed into a winter wonderland. And for some silly reason, Chloe's eyes filled with tears.

She'd received a standing ovation more times than she could count at Radio City Music Hall, one of the oldest and most storied theaters in the country. Never had it meant as much as this one did, though. Because this time, she wasn't made up to look exactly like the other thirty-five dancers onstage. She was simply herself, Chloe Wilde.

But that wasn't quite true, was it? Her name was Chloe Wilde Kent, and as her students danced and twirled in the swirling bits of snow, her husband was walking straight toward her through the parted crowd with two bouquets of red roses in his arms.

She froze, unable to move, unable to breathe. If this was some kind of wonderful Christmas daydream, she didn't want to know. She wanted to stay in this perfect, private snow globe forever, where she was surrounded by her family—and where that family included a little girl dressed in a nightgown and ballet slippers, and a man who never failed to take her breath away.

Anders bent to give one of the bouquets to Lolly. Then Chloe took her attention away from him long enough to lock eyes with Emily through the dizzying snow flurries, and her mother simply mouthed the words *I love you*, followed by *Merry Christmas*.

"I love you, too," Chloe whispered.

Merry Christmas, indeed.

Then Anders was right there, just inches away, with snow in his hair and a look in his eyes that was so reverent, so pure that her tears spilled over and streamed down her face.

He handed her the bouquet in his arms and said, "Don't cry, love," so softly that she could barely hear his lovely baritone above the strains of Tchaikovsky, mixed with the happy sounds of children, parents and grandparents. Of family.

And then Anders cupped her face, brushing her tears away with the pads of his thumbs. His hands smelled of winter and roses—so good and familiar that it was like being wrapped in a blanket. Then his face grew serious as he said, "I lied, Chloe. I don't want a clean break. Not now, not ever. I'm in love with you. There's nothing in this world more real than the feelings I have for you."

"I love you, too," she breathed.

There was so much to say, so many promises to make, but before she could utter another word, he dropped down on one knee and smiled up at her from the floor, now completely covered in white, like an upturned bowl of sugar.

He took her hand and kissed the diamond ring on her finger—the one she'd never take off again. "Will you stay married to me, Chloe? I know the proposal is a little late, but I never asked you properly the first time."

All around them, tiny ballerinas sprawled on the ground, waving their arms and legs, giggling and making snow angels. It didn't matter to them that the snow wasn't real or that they were in a ballet studio dressed in recital costumes instead of bundled up in frosty Central Park.

They believed.

Sometimes pretending was better than the real thing. Sometimes it was a precious, perfect gift.

"Yes." Chloe nodded. "I will absolutely stay married to you."

Anders rose to his feet to kiss her, and as her eyes drifted closed and his mouth came down on hers, warm and sweet, she was conscious of only one, overriding thought.

I believe, too.

She believed in love. She believed in Anders. She believed in *them*.

And for the first Christmas in a very long time, she believed in the magic of make-believe.

* * * * *

Be sure to check out the other Wilde Hearts books:

The Ballerina's Secret
How to Romance a Runaway Bride
The Bachelor's Baby Surprise

Available now from Harlequin Special Edition!

And look out for Teri Wilson's next book, the second book of the brand-new Furever Yours continuity,

Tucker to the Rescue

available in February 2019.

COMING NEXT MONTH FROM

HARLEQUIN®

SPECIAL EDITION

Available December 18, 2018

#2665 A DEAL MADE IN TEXAS

The Fortunes of Texas: The Lost Fortunes • by Michelle Major

It's like a scene from Christine Briscoe dreams when the flirtatious attorney asks her to be his (pretend) girlfriend. But there is nothing make-believe about the sparks between the quiet office manager and the sexy Fortune scion. Are they heading for heartbreak...or down the aisle?

#2666 THE COWBOY'S LESSON IN LOVE

Forever, Texas • by Marie Ferrarella

Ever since Clint Washburn's wife left, he's built up defenses to keep everyone in Forever out—including his son. Now the boy's teacher, Wynona Chee, is questioning his parenting! And Clint is experiencing feelings he thought long dead. Wynona has her homework cut out for her if she's going to teach this cowboy to love again.

#2667 A NEW LEASH ON LOVE

Furever Yours • by Melissa Senate

Army vet Matt Fielding is back home, figuring out his new normal. Goal one: find his niece the perfect puppy. He never expected to find the girl he'd left behind volunteering at the local shelter. Matt can't refuse Claire's offer of puppy training but will he be able to keep his emotional distance this time around?

#2668 THE LAWMAN'S CONVENIENT FAMILY

Rocking Chair Rodeo • by Judy Duarte

When Adam Santiago teams up with music therapist Julie Chapman to save two young orphans, pretty soon *his* heart's a goner, too! Julie's willing to do anything—even become Adam's pretend bride—to keep a brother and sister together. Will this marriage of convenience become an affair of the heart?

#2669 TWINS FOR THE SOLDIER

American Heroes • by Rochelle Alers

Army ranger Lee Remington didn't think he'd ever go back to Wickham Falls, home of some of his worst memories. But he's shocked by a powerful attraction to military widow Angela Mitchell. But as he preps for his ready-made family, there's one thing Lee forgot to tell her...

#2670 WINNING CHARLOTTE BACK

Sweet Briar Sweethearts • by Kathy Douglass

Dr. Rick Tyler just moved in next door to Charlotte Shields. She thought she'd seen the last of him when he abandoned her at the altar but he's determined to make the move work for his young son. Will he get a second chance with Charlotte in the bargain?

YOU CAN FIND MORE INFORMATION ON UPCOMING HARLEQUIN® TITLES, FREE EXCERPTS AND MORE AT WWW.HARLEQUIN.COM.

HSECNM1218

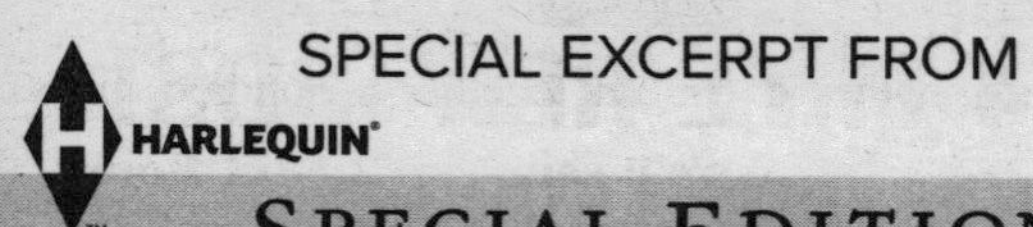

USA TODAY *bestselling author Judy Duarte's*
The Lawman's Convenient Family
is the story of Julie Chapman, a music therapist who needs a convenient husband in order to save two orphans from foster care. Lawman Adam Santiago fits the bill, but suddenly they both find themselves longing to become a family—forever!

Read on for a sneak preview of the next great book in the Rocking Chair Rodeo miniseries.

"Lisa," the man dressed as Zorro said, "I'd heard you were going to be here."

He clearly thought Julie was someone else. She probably ought to say something, but up close, the gorgeous bandito seemed to have stolen both her thoughts and her words.

"It's nice to finally meet you." His deep voice set her senses reeling. "I've never really liked blind dates."

Talk about masquerades and mistaken identities. Before Julie could set him straight, he took her hand in a polished, gentlemanly manner and kissed it. His warm breath lingered on her skin, setting off a bevy of butterflies in her tummy.

"Dance with me," he said.

Her lips parted, but for the life of her, she still couldn't speak, couldn't explain. And she darn sure couldn't object.

Zorro led her away from the buffet tables and to the dance floor. When he opened his arms, she again had the opportunity to tell him who she really was. But instead, she stepped into his embrace, allowing him to take the lead.

His alluring aftershave, something manly, taunted her. As she savored his scent, as well as the warmth of his muscular arms, her pulse soared. She leaned her head on his shoulder as they swayed to a sensual beat, their movements in perfect accord, as though they'd danced together a hundred times before.

Now would be a good time to tell him she wasn't Lisa, but she seemed to have fallen under a spell that grew stronger with every beat of the music. The moment turned surreal, like she'd stepped into a fairy tale with a handsome rogue.

Once again, she pondered revealing his mistake and telling him her name, but there'd be time enough to do that after the song ended. Then she'd return to the kitchen, slipping off like Cinderella. But instead of a glass slipper, she'd leave behind her momentary enchantment.

But several beats later, a cowboy tapped Zorro on the shoulder. "I need you to come outside."

Zorro looked at him and frowned. "Can't you see I'm busy?"

The cowboy, whose outfit was so authentic he seemed to be the real deal, rolled his eyes.

Julie wished she could have worn her street clothes. Would now be a good time to admit that she wasn't an actual attendee but here to work at the gala?

"What's up?" Zorro asked.

The cowboy folded his arms across his chest and shifted his weight to one hip. "Someone just broke into my pickup."

Zorro's gaze returned to Julie. "I'm sorry, Lisa. I'm going to have to morph into cop mode."

Now it was Julie's turn to tense. He was actually a police officer in real life? A slight uneasiness settled over her, an old habit she apparently hadn't outgrown. Not that she had any real reason to fear anyone in law enforcement nowadays.

HSEEXP1218